DEFENDING THE PLAYER

PIERSON U BOOK 3

ELOUISE TYNAN

ARDENTLY ROMANCE

This book is a work of fiction. All characters, organisations, and events portrayed in the novel are either productions of the author's imagination or are used fictitiously.

DEFENDING THE PLAYER

Edited: Amy Maranville at Kracken Communications

Cover Design: Sarah Paige at the Book Cover Boutique

Cover image: Michelle Lancaster @lanefotograf

Cover model: Lochie Carey

Published by Ardently Romance

Ebook: 978-0-6457512-2-2

Paperback: 978-0-6457512-3-9

To all the girls who fiercely guard their hearts...
this one is for you

ONE

IMOGEN

"I CAN'T STAND YOU," I growled, gripping the edge of the table and leaning forward.

A satisfied smile spread across Bant's face, blue eyes sparkling with amusement. "Tell me more. Because when you lean over the table like that I can see straight down your dress."

I scowled standing upright and crossing my arms over my chest. There were few people who infuriated me more than the pretty boy basketball player standing across from me.

I motioned to the game of beer pong laid out in front of us. "You're a cheat."

His expression washed with disbelief. "The aim of the game is to get the tiny ball in the cup. How exactly did I cheat?"

"You're like seven foot and you lean halfway across the

table to take your shots, which means you're practically in spitting distance of the cup."

He scoffed, somehow managing to look more attractive as he did it. He was all honeyed hair, broad shoulders and lean muscle from endless basketball training. But it was his permanently self-assured smile that irked me the most, as though he were all too aware that there wasn't a student on this campus he couldn't charm out of their pants with nothing but a grin. It was annoying as hell.

Especially when I'd sworn to loathe him for the rest of my life.

He raised a brow, that penetrating blue gaze unsettling me in all kinds of ways I wasn't remotely willing to examine. "I didn't lean. I don't need to cheat to get you drunk, Sweets."

"Don't call me that, jackass."

We scowled at each other.

"Kick his butt, Im!" my best friend Stella called from the other side of the busy room where she was helping Bant's teammate, Davis, and our other best friend, Monty, stack empty beer cans in some kind of fort around a passed-out Hooker, a junior on the team.

As Bant and I continued to glare at each other, the smitten blonde in a green dress who had been hanging around him like dog poop on his shoe for most of the night glanced between us with a confused expression.

"Wait, do you hear that?" Bant cupped a hand to his ear. "I think it's Satan calling his hellhound home."

He gave me a pointed look, followed by that infuriating smirk I wanted to slap off his annoyingly perfect face.

The blonde giggled behind her drink.

I'm pretty sure he could have said he was off to stab his grandmother and she would have laughed like he was a stand-up comic on tour. The girl was clearly dying to get into his pants. But then, as a campus basketball star, Luke Bantempelli was never short of women lining up to ride him. Or men, for that matter.

He nodded at me. "Come on, Sweets, you know I deserve the point."

"You deserve syphilis."

Grabbing the cup from the table, I tossed the soaked ping pong ball in his direction and knocked back the shot of beer, enjoying the surprise that washed over his face.

"Fuck me, did you actually just concede?"

"You know, you should really see a professional about how obsessed you are with the sound of your own voice."

His eyes glinted with playful challenge. "You're studying psych, aren't you? Let's do a session, Doc. Preferably naked."

I rolled my eyes, annoyance searing through me that he'd bested me in this little verbal sparring match. I wasn't too proud to admit I'd lost sleep over it the handful of times he'd managed to walk away after one-upping me during one of our tense interactions.

His blue eyes studied me, glinting with knowing victory. "You're hot when you're mad."

"Go write poetry about it, playboy." I gestured to the game. "Are you going to take your shot or are you not done ogling me like a creep?"

His gaze raked slowly over my body, taking in my tight red wrap dress. I fought hard to keep my cheeks from flaming the same color at his obvious perusal.

"Now I'm done." He grinned, holding up the ball and lining up his shot. "You'll be drunk by the end of the night."

I shot him a sickly sweet smile. "We'll see about that."

TWO

BANT

TURNS out I was the one who was drunk by the end of the night.

Monty had joined Imogen and the two of them had kicked my ass at beer pong. Imogen had relished every second of it, her gloating smile irritating and making my dick twitch in my jeans all at the same time. She was a mouthy pain in the ass, but that didn't stop me from wanting that mouth anywhere on my body. From the second she'd crashed into my life with Monty and Stella, I'd imagined what it would be like to have her riding me.

She'd probably tell me what a hopeless fuck boy I was the entire time, but hell if I didn't like the sound of that scenario.

Only instead of gently wooing her into bed with me tonight like I'd been trying to do for more than a year now, I'd downed too many beers and tequila shots with my team-mates. Imogen was long gone and I was in the spare room downstairs, pinned against the closed door with the cute blonde with giant tits wrapped around me.

Ever since Reggie moved out last year and the rest of us had refused to let any of the no-chill freshman or sophomores on the team move in, Reg's room had been turned into a hook up spot at every party.

"You're so hot, I've wanted to sleep with you for so long," the blonde said, sucking on my neck, her voice breathy with lust.

I *really* needed to remember her name, but my beer and tequila-boggled brain was giving me nothing.

"Well, here we are..." I said, with a chuckle.

She pulled back, giving me a sultry smile, before she slid down my body to unzip my jeans, pushing them down my legs.

I'd forgotten to pack underwear in my sports bag after practice and had been too lazy to change when I'd gotten home, so I was going commando. My hard dick sprang free, practically slapping her in the face. She squeaked in surprise before wrapping her hand around my shaft and staring up at me, closing her lips around the tip.

I let out a groan and tipped my head back against the door as she swallowed me down.

Is there anything better than a blow job?

The answer was no. Absolutely nothing.

The blonde moved her lips and tongue over me in all the right ways. She worked me over for several minutes in what was near-perfect technique, and it felt great, but...

I frowned down at her. "I can't believe I'm about to say this, but this isn't working for me."

She pulled back, affronted.

"No, no, it's me. You're great. You're doing some killer work down there."

She stroked my shaft as she stared up at me. "So, what's the problem?"

Imogen. That was the goddamn problem.

We couldn't be in the same room without sniping at each other like sexually frustrated teenagers, but it didn't mean my dick didn't want to know her smart mouth intimately. And I couldn't get her off my fucking mind. There was a hot girl down on her knees blowing me like it was her only goal in life and I was thinking about someone who looked at me like she wouldn't spit on me if I was on fire.

Yet something about that hatred in her eyes got me hard.

I wanted her. *Fucking badly.*

"Maybe you could scowl and call me a jackass or something?"

The blonde frowned, starting to edge away.

"No, wait... just forget it," I said, thrusting into her hand. "This is great, you're doing great."

She gave me a small smile and took my cock in her mouth again.

My head fell back against the door and I closed my eyes, picturing a scowling girl with sultry lips and dark hair sucking me off.

I came hard.

THREE

IMOGEN

"MOM AND DAD ARE FIGHTING AGAIN."

My younger sister's voice echoed down the phone and I sighed.

Slipping through the door just inside the psych building, I listened as she shared yet another story about our once-happily married parents now fighting like opposing dictators waging war over a secret oil supply.

"It's the third time this week," Lola went on. "They've locked themselves away in Mom's office thinking I can't hear them, but they're shouting so loud I'm pretty sure the neighbors are enjoying the show."

My little sister was the only one left at home. She was a senior in high school and counting down the months until she could leave for college — she was thrilled when she got early acceptance to Pierson for the fall. She couldn't wait to get out of that house.

My parents hadn't always been this way. Growing up,

they seemed like a couple so in love, raising their three daughters in suburban Connecticut and giving us everything we'd ever needed. But in the past year, something had changed. I knew it was stressing Lola out, which meant it was stressing me out. I hated seeing my little sister upset.

"I'm really sorry, Lo." I stopped outside my behavioral psychology class, standing out of the way of the other students trickling in. "I know it sucks at home right now. Hopefully Mom and Dad sort their stuff out soon. I have to go to class, but I'll call you tonight, okay?"

"Sure, Im. Talk to you later."

I ended the call and sent a text to my older sister, Naomi, who was studying economics at Brown.

ME: *Mom and Dad fighting again. Lola says it's getting worse. Time for an intervention?*

I headed into the lecture hall, sliding into a seat beside my friend Carly, as my phone buzzed.

NAOMI: *Ugh. Again? I'll call Lola after my classes.*

"Everything okay?" Carly asked, frowning at me.

I slid my phone into my bag, pulling out my laptop and slapping a smile on my face. "All fine, just chatting to my sisters."

I didn't need to broadcast my family drama unnecessarily. Hopefully it was just a rough patch for my parents. An increasingly *prolonged* rough patch.

They used to be the poster couple for a perfect marriage. What the hell had happened to send things so far off course? My track record with relationships was a joke, but I'd always held out hope that one day I'd find something as pure and true as what my parents had.

The fact that all seemed to be unravelling was unnerving. If they couldn't make it work, what hope did I have?

The professor strolled into the room, kicking off the

lecture, declaring today's session would be full of very useful information we'd need for an upcoming assignment. I had to do well in this class, so I sat up straighter, taking detailed notes and paying attention.

The time went by fast and I was deep in concentration when a ball of paper hit me in the shoulder. Carly and I both swivelled, looking for the asshole who was throwing projectiles like we were in the fifth grade.

Jackson Marin, a cocky lacrosse jerk, offered me a self-assured grin from two rows back.

"Read it," he mouthed, slouching back in his seat and man-spreading like arrogance personified.

Man-spreading in a lecture hall should be illegal.

Carly picked up the ball of paper and handed it to me. I opened it, rolling my eyes when I read the words.

Going to finally agree to go out with me this week?

I tipped my head back, fighting the urge to groan in the quiet lecture hall.

Jackson had asked me out several times last year and I'd knocked him back every time. I had zero interest in dating right now, mostly due to my hideously bad track record when it came to choosing guys. I'd been cheated on not once, not twice, but three times. First by one of my high school boyfriends, then by a random guy at Pierson, who, in hindsight, I wasn't even that into, but it still stung.

The most recent cheating asshole was my last boyfriend, Bobby. He'd been studying nursing at U of M and I'd been falling hard for him. It was around the same time I realized my feelings for him were getting serious that I learned he'd been studying the naked bodies of most of his female classmates back in his dorm while he'd been dating me.

I was starting to think the problem was most definitely me. Or at least... my pecker picker.

Guys sucked and I was done with them. My judgment couldn't be trusted. I was committed to focusing on myself, my goals and my future this year.

I glanced at the note from Jackson. If only I were a smoker, I could pull out a lighter, set the paper in my hand on fire and send a clear message to Jackson that his advances were unwanted and completely fruitless. Apparently, me saying it repeatedly to his face wasn't enough.

But smoking had never appealed to me, so I settled for scrunching the paper up and tossing it in my bag, ignoring Jackson completely in favor of my notes.

It wasn't that Jackson was hideous; he was decent enough to look at. It was his personality that sucked. By all accounts he thought being on the lacrosse team made him some kind of campus superstar, worthy of worship from any girl he came across. His fragile ego couldn't comprehend how or why I wasn't interested.

His ego didn't make sense. It wasn't like he was on the basketball team. Not that I'd date a basketball player either....

Bant's face flashed in my mind and I shoved it aside.

Hell no. No way.

I'd rather have seven root canals and a smear test for good measure than deal with Bant's ego for more than a minute. And with the rate he hooked up, there would be no possibility of a meaningful relationship, even if I *wanted* one. Which I didn't.

"You okay?" Carly whispered, eyeing me. "Jackson's a pain in the ass. Want me to sort him out for you?"

I couldn't help my smile. Carly might be petite but she packed one hell of a punch. I'd seen it once when a drunk guy had pawed her at a frat party and she'd sent him sprawling. It was in that moment I'd known we were going to be friends.

"Jackson doesn't really want to date me. He just doesn't like that I don't want to date him. He can't comprehend that someone wouldn't want him."

When the professor called for the end of the lecture, we packed up our stuff, heading for the door. I made sure to avoid even glancing in Jackson's direction so he wouldn't talk to me.

"I've got to run, I've got a lunch date with a cute science nerd," Carly said, wiggling her eyebrows.

I waved goodbye, so distracted that I failed to see the five foot eight inches of arrogance standing in front of me.

"Imogen, Imogen, Imogen..."

The drawling voice stopped me, Jackson leaning against the wall like a living stereotype of a nineties movie bad boy. And not the appealing kind.

I sighed, gripping the straps of my book bag. "What do you want, Jackson?"

His eyes dropped down to my legs and I instantly regretted wearing a skirt today.

"You know what I want."

"Yeah, well... I'm not interested in getting you off."

He smirked like my reluctance entertained him. "And just why not? Plenty of girls would love a night with me."

I gestured down the hall. "Then why don't you go find one of them?"

He pushed off the wall and moved closer. I raised my chin and held my ground, refusing to concede a step for this idiot.

"Because I want the one in front of me. She's hot and fiery and there's no good reason for her shutting me down."

I opened my mouth to reply that I didn't need a reason beyond the word no, when a heavy arm landed across my shoulders and I was tucked against a warm and distinctly toned body. "Yeah, there is. Because she's with me."

Jackson's gaze shot up to the six-foot-plus ball player now claiming me, while I resisted the urge to elbow Bant in the ribs.

"Bantempelli." Jackson's jaw clenched, but he forced himself to be civil. "How's it going, man?"

I ground my teeth at Bant's interference. Why was he even in the psychology building at this time of day? We were nowhere near the basketball stadium. Or any of the sororities.

"It'd be going better if you stopped hitting on my girl."

I resisted the urge to roll my eyes. How the hell had I found myself stuck in the middle of this pathetic male posturing? All I wanted to do was go to my next class, not be forced to witness the ego games of two campus peacocks.

Then again, if it momentarily got Jackson off my ass maybe I'd let it play out.

"Your girl?" Jackson's gaze darted between me and Bant. "Since when?"

Bant shrugged and I slapped a docile smile on my face that physically pained me.

"Since now."

Jackson's gaze ran over me with what looked like regret, then he raised his palms and backed away. "I didn't know, dude."

Bant smiled back. "Well, now you do."

It annoyed me to no end that when I'd rebuffed him, Jackson had taken it as an invitation to keep trying. But a few words from Bant and suddenly he was backing off.

I watched Jackson go, the moment he pushed through the door and disappeared I shoved Bant away.

He stumbled, chuckling. "Is that the thanks I get for saving you?"

"Saving me? I had it covered." I started down the hall, righteous indignation boiling inside me. Other girls may be all too willing to fall for Luke Bantempelli's brand of easy charm, but I wasn't buying it. He was a monumental pain in my ass.

My sour mood didn't stop him from following after me.

"What are you doing?" I snapped.

"Walking my girl to class."

I rounded on him. "I'm not your girl. While I maybe, vaguely, appreciate you getting Jackson off my case, if you think we're about to play out some kind of fake dating scenario like Monty and West had going on, you're delusional. I'd rather pick out my fingernails with a butter knife than pretend to be your girlfriend for more than the minute I just had it forced on me."

A stupid grin spread across his face. "You're really intense, you know that?"

I shook my head, heading for the door. This time he didn't follow me.

"Glad I could amuse you," I called back, pushing through the doors and leaving Luke Bantempelli in my rearview where he belonged.

FOUR

BANT

"LUKE!" a small voice called my name the moment I stepped through the door of the women's shelter. Kelsie ran up to me and wrapped her small arms around my waist.

"What's going on, kid? You being good for your mom?"

I glanced up at Renee who was sitting at one of the tables in the giant dining hall. I'd been coming to volunteer at the women's shelter in town since my freshman year at Pierson. Renee was one of the first women I'd met here, back when Kelsie had only been two. I'd watched the kid grow up and she'd wormed her way into my heart with her witty anecdotes and sweet observations. Now we were the best of friends. I loved the way her little face lit up whenever I came to serve at the shelter.

My connection to this place was why the team had raised money for the shelter last year with the player auction. But coming here wasn't about padding out my college transcript or making me feel like a good person. This place was personal to me and why I'd willingly jumped through every hoop I had to in order to get special permission to volunteer here.

"Are you here to help with dinner?" Kelsie asked, her wide brown eyes staring up at me.

"Sure am, kid. And I brought you something."

A smile stretched across her little face as I pulled a giant Snickers bar from the back pocket of my jeans.

She took it, eyes wide. "This is for me?"

I nodded. "Of course. I wouldn't bring candy for just anyone. Only my number one girl."

She grinned at me, running back to her mom to show her the candy bar.

I knew what it was like to spend time living in a shelter like Kelsie and Renee.

My mom and I had stayed in a shelter just like this one back in upstate New York when she'd finally found the courage to leave my deadbeat abusive father. I'd been eight years old when we'd moved into the shelter, and the people who worked or volunteered there helped change the course of our lives. My mom was the strongest woman I'd ever known for the choices she'd made to save us. And those volunteers had helped her do it.

Now she was a successful executive assistant, living in a modest yet comfortable apartment in New York City. And I was living my dream at Pierson.

I wanted to help families just like us. That's why I turned up to the shelter two or three times a week, depending on how many extra practices Coach forced on us.

"Sorry I'm late, man," Davis said, hustling through the door and clapping me on the shoulder. "Had to stay back after class to talk about my paper."

"All good, I just got here. Let's hit the kitchens."

We cut through the tables of the dining hall, and I waved at Renee as we passed, heading for the industrial spaces at the back. The smell of roasted vegetables and cooked meat wafted through the doors.

Davis had been my friend since we were freshman and joined the basketball team the same year. The guy may be a show-boating player both on and off the court, but he had a big heart he didn't show most people. The second he'd learned about my time at the shelter he'd offered to join me and, after going through the same rigorous screening process I'd done, had come with me ever since. He was the kind of friend every guy needed.

West and Van had come along too, whenever their schedules allowed. But now they were both off living the NBA dream in Washington and New York.

Raven, the woman in charge of the kitchens, tossed aprons and hairnets at us the moment we strolled in, putting us to work prepping the food. An hour later, we were out in the dining hall, serving it up to the lines of people waiting to be fed.

I smiled at each person, making small talk as I spooned mashed potato and green beans onto their plates.

"I had lunch with a bunch of the lacrosse guys today..." Davis said, piling slices of roast beef on the plate of the woman in front of him. "Jackson had some interesting things to say."

"I find that hard to believe. The most interesting thing about the guy is when he leaves."

Davis snorted. "He seems to think you and Imogen are dating."

I sighed. "He was giving her a hard time. I may have stepped in and told him to back off because she was mine."

Davis outright laughed this time. "Dude, you're so whipped for that girl and she doesn't want a damn thing to do with you."

"I'm not whipped. I'm just a sucker for a killer body and I want her to hold hers against me. Her smart mouth doesn't hurt, either."

There was no point wondering if I could want more than that with a girl like Imogen. Or any girl for that matter. I had a history of falling way too hard, way too fast and after what had happened with my first college girlfriend, Delaney, my freshman year at Pierson, I'd sworn off those kinds of feelings for the foreseeable future. If that disastrous attempt at a relationship had taught me anything, it was to play it cool and keep it casual. That philosophy had served me well the past few years. Now I never got attached and they didn't either.

It definitely broke my mother's heart that I hadn't brought a girl home since high school, when all she wanted was to see me settled with someone. But college wasn't the place for that. Not when there was an endless parade of girls willing to bone down on any given day. So I wanted to add Imogen to that roster. Was that a crime?

The fact she loathed me made these little games we played all the more the fun.

Davis grinned like he didn't believe a word of it. "Whatever you say, bro."

The line shuffled along, and soon Renee, Kelsie's mom, was standing in front of me. She smiled but it didn't quite reach her eyes.

"All okay today, Renee?"

She bit the inside of her cheek, nodding.

Something was definitely off. I'd known Renee and

Kelsie a long time now and Renee was usually just as engaging and upbeat as her daughter.

I lowered my voice. "Something weighing on you?"

She glanced at the person behind in her line, then back at me. "It's Kelsie's dad. The shelter director told me he's been sniffing around, trying to find us. I'm worried he might turn up here."

My shoulders stiffened, my spine turning rigid. This shelter was a safe haven for so many like Renee and Kelsie — and like my mom and I — who had run from violent lives, desperate to escape. The last thing Renee needed was her hateful ex finding her when she was finally free and trying to start over.

"If he turns up here, you call me. I don't care if I'm in class or practice, I'll be here." I took in her worried expression, hands fidgeting with her plate. "You still have my number?"

She nodded. "Thank you, Luke. Hopefully it doesn't come to that."

I spooned mashed potatoes onto her plate, grabbing an extra and adding some for Kelsie.

She gave my wrist an affectionate squeeze before taking them. "Does your mother know what a good man you are?"

I smiled back at her. "Who do you think raised me this way?"

FIVE

IMOGEN

"IT'S FRIDAY NIGHT, and what do we do on Fridays?" Monty asked, raising her glass to mine and Stella's.

"Dress up slutty and drink too much?" I offered with a sly smile.

"Exactly!" Stella cheered, clinking our glasses and knocking back her lemon drop shot.

I followed suit, the citrus liquor both sweet and sour on the way down. We were parked in a booth at O'Reilly's, the best bar close to campus, after we'd watched the Pierson basketball boys win their home game against Michigan State.

Monty discarded her glass on the table. "Speaking of slutty, did you see the pictures of West photographed with his teammates and a bunch of girls at that Wizards charity event last night?"

Stella rolled her eyes. "Please, you know West wouldn't have given them a lick of attention."

I tried and failed to hold back my laugh. "Not when you're bombarding him with naked video chat requests every second day."

Monty had decided getting naked was a good way to keep her long-distance, NBA-playing boyfriend's attention. Not that she needed to try. West was obsessed with her and had been since they first met. But I guess Monty never got to see just how devastated he'd been as he'd sat beside her in the hospital after everything that went down with Alec in sophomore year. That boy wasn't going anywhere then and he still wasn't now, no matter how many women threw themselves at him because he was a pro ball player.

"How do you stay so chilled about the whole NBA circus?" Monty asked Stella.

She shrugged. "I trust Van. And if he's going to cheat on me, he doesn't deserve me."

Stella was notoriously laidback and level-headed, a lot like her boyfriend Van. They were also intensely private, the two of them having first hooked up when Stella was a freshman, something she'd managed to keep a secret from both Monty and I until last year, when Van had broken up with his girlfriend and quietly pursued Stella until he won her over.

She twirled her glass on the table top, those green eyes that drove guys wild landing on me. "How's it going with the guy you met at the campus bookshop?"

I sighed. He'd been a promising prospect when we'd first swapped numbers, texting me consistently and asking to catch up for coffee or a drink. But when I'd had to knock him back because I'd been busy with classes, he'd gone quiet. Just another reason I was swearing off relationships this year. The boys on this campus were more trouble than they were worth with their rejection issues or emotional baggage.

I shrugged. "The slower his replies are, the hotter his friends get."

"Brutal," Davis said, appearing at the booth with a grin and sliding in beside Monty, hip-checking her to get her to shuffle over. She gave him a playful swat but did as he asked, sliding closer to Stella. Hooker, Bant and Hernandez followed, Bant sliding into the booth next to me. I edged away from him, determined to ignore the perpetual human thorn in my side, even as my stomach clenched at the sight of him.

No, I instructed myself. *Absolutely not. Don't even think about it.*

"What are we talking about?" Hernandez asked.

"Imogen's dating life," Monty offered.

Hooker took a sip of his drink. "And what have we concluded?"

I sighed. "That I'm attracted to assholes with the emotional depth of a puddle."

Bant snorted beside me. "It's because you wouldn't know a real man if he dropped down and sucked your toes."

"You offering, Bantempelli?" Davis challenged, hiding his grin behind his glass.

Bant's smile was beyond smug. "At least she'd be guaranteed to leave satisfied."

"Wow, impaling myself on your wonder cock will really change my life that much, huh? Someone is sure of himself."

He slid me a sideways glance, taking a sip of his beer. "I'm yet to hear a complaint from the girls who leave my bedroom."

"Really? I'm surprised you can remember them all, let alone remember to poll them on their way out."

I shifted further away from him. As much as I was loathe to admit anything favorable about him, the smell of his cologne was tantalizing enough to get me pregnant.

"Men are so much easier to please," Davis offered.

Stella laughed. "So, what's your perfect woman then, Davis?"

"Easy." He offered up his trademark Davis grin. "Makes me food and has a decent rack."

"Bro, did you just describe your mother?" Hooker asked, and I couldn't help the laugh that burst out of me.

Davis's expression darkened. "You did not just talk about my mama's rack."

"To be fair, dude, your mom is smoking hot."

Hooker looked to Bant for support, but he pressed his lips together and shook his head.

"That's it, I need another drink!" Davis slid from the booth and headed for the bar. It took all of twenty-three seconds before a girl sidled up to him and any thoughts of his mom and his teammates were forgotten.

Family was the last thing I wanted to think about right now. Lola had texted me more times than I could count over the past week about the deteriorating state of our parents' marriage. It weighed heavily on me and I wasn't the one who had to live under the same roof as them or bear witness to their near-constant bickering. I needed to get Lola away from them for a while. A visit to Pierson to hang out with me, Monty and Stella was the perfect solution.

I was pulling my phone from my purse to text my sister when a heavy arm landed across my shoulders, Bant smiling down at me.

"Monty and Stella were showing their team spirit at the

game tonight in their Pierson basketball shirts. What's it going to take to get you into a jersey?"

"A lobotomy," I deadpanned.

His eyes sparked with amusement. "I'd rather find out what it'll take to get you out of it anyway."

I shoved him off and his arm slid from my shoulders as he chuckled.

"If it's *you* trying to get me out of it... then also a lobotomy."

He dropped his voice so only I could hear, that cocky grin playing on his mouth.

"We both know you want me, Im. All that pent-up hostility is just a cover for how much you're dying to meet my disco stick."

I gagged. "Actually, I can't stand you. But I can see how small minds could miss that when I'm always so subtle about it."

"What can't you stand about Bantempelli?" Hernandez called across the table. "Look at that face."

All eyes were on Bant and he winked, like he knew he was a prize girls across campus were willing to auction off their own dignity for. Sure, the dirty blond hair and the bright blue eyes on a killer basketball body might be difficult to resist, but his irritatingly self-assured personality shut down any thoughts of letting him know it. Or ever getting it on with him.

I screwed up my nose. "It's the arrogance for me."

Or maybe it was because he was the poster boy for every guy who had ever cheated on me. There was little difference between the guys who'd wronged me and Bant, a guy who made his way through women faster than he went through toilet paper. I wasn't about to be another one he humped and dumped without a second thought.

Bant tried and failed to look affronted. "You wound me, Imogen."

I held back a snort. "I'm pretty sure there's nothing in this world that could wound that ego of yours. It's impenetrable."

"Just like your pants, apparently."

I scowled. "You're a real charmer, did anyone ever tell you that?"

"And you're kind of a shrew. Did anyone ever tell you that?" he cut back.

"Children, children, please!" Monty said, throwing her hands out to silence us. "Not at the dinner table."

I sat back, shaking my head and refusing to look at him. "I need a drink."

Only one drink wouldn't cut it.

I'd have to down a whole keg if I was going to get through another night stuck with Bant and his annoyingly arrogant bullshit.

SIX

BANT

"DUDE, can you focus? We're getting reamed here," Hooker called.

No.

No, I could not.

We were playing a game of three-on-three on the gym courts at the back of campus, something the guys and I liked to do on weekends. The games were always chill and involved more showboating and trick shots than Coach would ever let us get away with at practice.

I was teamed up with Hooker and Jericho against Davis, Hernandez and Li, but I was failing to hit shot after shot because I couldn't concentrate for shit.

Monty, Stella, and Imogen had turned up about twenty minutes ago, yoga mats in hand, ready to get their zen on. Or chi. Or whatever the hell people got on during yoga.

It was distracting enough that Imogen had strolled by the court to the rec room next door in a pair of dark green exercise shorts that clung to her apple of an ass and had me fantasizing about sinking my teeth into it. Or spanking it all night long. She was currently doing some intense stretch, bent in half, with her ass up in the air, and I couldn't tear my eyes away from the windows.

I could barely remember where the hell I was, let alone how to shoot the ball.

Fuck, I'm in trouble.

The girl didn't just have an incredible ass, she was also a pain in the ass. But damn if I could stop thinking about getting her into bed. I was so focused on Imogen's smooth legs and perfect body. What would it feel like to walk up behind her, grip her hips to pull her against me and hear her moan my name?

I was so lost in my dirty mind that when Jericho pitched the ball at me, it hit me square in the chest, bouncing off.

"Bro, come on!" Jeri called, jogging after Li, who had snagged the ball after my mistake and was halfway down the court already.

"Tell me again how you're not into her," Davis said with a laugh.

I wasn't into her. I wanted to sleep with her, there was a difference.

I was well aware of my tendency to get attached. There was no way in hell I'd ever be making that mistake again. But that didn't mean I'd turn down the opportunity to get naked with Imogen and have the sweatiest, dirtiest time of our lives.

Dragging my eyes away from the spank-bank worthy sight in front of me, I bolted down the other end of the court to defend Hernandez as he took a shot, swiping the rebound and hustling to the other end to put up a shot. Davis was right there with me, knocking it away before it could hit the ring, the ball bouncing across the court and hitting the rec room window.

"Sorry ladies," he called out. "Bant couldn't hit a shot to save his mama today."

I gave him a friendly shove as Imogen stood tall from her latest stretch, coming out to grab the ball and stalking across the court with it propped under her arm.

"The hoop's that way." She pointed up at it like I was slow and she was explaining a basic concept to me.

"Thanks for the tip. You know, you could go do your bendy shit somewhere else."

She pulled a face and, despite the evident loathing behind it, it made me a little hard.

"Bendy shit? If you expanded your horizons beyond basketball and licking everything in a skirt, you might know basic things like what yoga is and how to do it."

"Jealous of where my tongue's been, Sweets?" I winked at her, purely because I knew it would piss her off. "If you want it between your legs, all you have to do is ask."

Her neck flushed red with anger, and she tossed the ball to Davis, giving me a hard once over. "I'd rather weld on a steel chastity belt for life than have your tongue anywhere near me, playboy."

She turned back to her friends, perfect ass swinging as she went.

"Try to get it in the right hole this time, Bantempelli," she called over her shoulder.

Fuck me, the girl was something else.

SEVEN

IMOGEN

"COME ON, Stell, please come in the Haunted House with me?"

She shook her head as we strolled around the Halloween carnival on campus, sharing a stick of cotton candy.

"No freaking way. You know how scared I get at things jumping out at me. Especially in the dark."

"You're really going to make me go in there alone?"

She pulled a face, tugging another piece of fluff from the stick and popping it in her mouth. "Don't do that, you're making me feel bad."

"Imagine how bad you'll feel when I'm accosted by a psycho in a Freddie Kruger mask with no one there to save me."

She pursed her lips, glancing around as she waged an internal war inside her head.

I was cruel for asking her to come when I knew how

much she hated that kind of stuff. But watching her lose her mind inside the Haunted House every year was all part of why coming to the carnival was so fun.

My phone vibrated in my pocket and I slid it out, staring at my mom's number on the screen. I'd avoided her when she'd called me two days ago. I was always the dutiful daughter who answered when my mother called, which meant she must be worried by my silence by now.

"Your mom again?" Stella asked.

I nodded, rejecting the call and sliding the phone back in my pocket.

"You can't avoid what's going on at home forever, Im. You need to speak to her eventually."

I sighed. "I know, just not today. My family has always been so close and my parents' relationship was so solid. I'm not ready to face the prospect that it might all be about to fall apart."

Stella squeezed my hand. "You don't know that's going to happen. Maybe Lola had it wrong and there's a reasonable explanation for their arguments."

"Maybe there is. I just don't want to think about any of it right now."

She nodded, something catching her eye over my shoulder.

"Look, here come the guys," she said, a triumphant smile spreading across her face. "Surely one of them will go in the Haunted House with you, which means I'm off the hook."

I glanced over my shoulder, Davis, Bant, Li, and Hooker were strolling through the crowd. Davis had a curvy brunette tucked at his side and Bant stopped to duck his head and listen to the blonde tugging on his arm, desperate for his attention. It was the same girl who'd hung off his every word the night Monty and I had beat him at beer pong.

I turned away, trying to fight a scowl.

Stella eyed me. "What's going on with you and Bant? The tension between you two seems to have gone up about eighty notches lately."

"Trust me when I say there's absolutely nothing going on. I'm just not in the mood for his insane basketball ego right now."

She opened her mouth to reply, an amused smile on her face like she didn't believe me, but she was cut off by Bant's booming voice, directed at her.

"Well, if it isn't my favorite lady of hooper house." He stopped, giving me a once over. "And Imogen."

He tugged on my ponytail just to piss me off.

Have we reverted all the way back to grade school now?

I swatted him away. "I'm surprised to see you out here, Bantempelli. I figured with that hideous face of yours they would have offered you a job in the Haunted House scaring the kiddies."

Davis chuckled. "You're savage, Im."

He held out a hand for a high-five, which I returned, earning me a scathing look from the girl at his side.

She had nothing to worry about. Cocky ball players weren't my style, even if Davis looked like Michael B. Jordan's younger brother. She could ride the whole team if she wanted to, I wouldn't stand in her way.

"Speaking of Haunted Houses, Imogen's dying to go inside but I refuse." Stella visibly shuddered. "One of you man mountains will escort her, right?"

"Errr... not really my scene," Li offered, his face draining of color.

Davis had lost interest in the conversation and was now

busy trying to get his tongue so far down the brunette's throat he could taste what she ate for lunch. And Hooker took that moment to become deeply engrossed in his phone.

What a bunch of babies.

"I'll do it," Bant piped up and my head snapped in his direction.

The blonde looked deeply put out at the suggestion and shook her head. "There's no way I'm going in."

"You don't need to come, babe," Bant said to her, his eyes glinting as he stared at me.

"That's okay, I don't need to go in," I said, backpedalling.

Stella shot me a look. "You've spent the past fifteen minutes trying to convince me what a good time it'll be." She shooed us towards the entrance. "You wanted a freaky friend and now you have one. Get in there."

Resigned, I stalked to the Haunted House, Bant following behind. Thankfully the line was short, but that didn't stop the awkward silence that hung between us while we waited.

It was interrupted by the eager blonde appearing again, running a finger down the arm of Bant's jacket. "Maybe when you're done, we can go on the Ferris wheel together?"

He gave her a forced smile. "Uh... sure."

I leaned around Bant. "Don't bet on it, hon. There's every chance he'll be sliced up by a chainsaw-wielding zombie in here and won't come out again."

The blonde looked scandalized. "Why would you say something like that?"

I shrugged. "My mother taught me to have dreams. My dream is to see Luke Bantempelli chopped up into tiny pieces."

Bant chuckled as the line moved up. "Don't listen to

her. This shit is just the she-devil's foreplay, she's super turned on right now."

Before the blonde could reply, the guy running the Haunted House ushered us forward, motioning to the entrance.

I turned to Bant. "I'm going to let you know now all bets are off once we step through those doors. If it comes down to it, I'll leave you for dead if I need to."

His responding chuckle shivered over my skin. "I'd expect nothing less from you, Sweets."

The door slammed behind us and we found ourselves standing in a pitch-black room and I instantly regretted my eagerness to do this.

This is fine. Totally fine.

There was a part of me that enjoyed being utterly terrified and another part that hated every minute of it. One of my psych professors called it being overridden by your sensation-seeking trait.

"Bant?" I hissed in the darkness, trying to keep the edge from my voice.

"I'm here."

His tone was casual, like we were simply taking a stroll in the park.

A black light started to flicker about twenty feet away, lighting up the hallway in front of us, all black walls and floor closing us in.

"Shall we?"

Bant motioned for me to go first, the black light illuminating his straight, white teeth as he grinned.

I pushed my shoulders back. "Okay, let's do this."

I'd taken a mere five steps down the hallway when a bloodied woman with wild hair, a small axe and a crazed look in her eyes, lunged at me from a hole in the wall.

I screamed and stumbled back into Bant's chest. His warm hands landed on my shoulders to steady me, giving a gentle squeeze that did nothing to level out my suddenly thundering heart rate.

He ducked down, lips caressing my ear. "Who knew you were a screamer?"

I shook him off, edging around the axe-wielding nut job. "There are a lot of things you don't know about me, and will never get to experience."

I didn't miss his amused smile in the flickering light.

We moved further into the maze of rooms and hallways, and I tried to play it cool as creeps wielding bloodied knives or manic clowns jumped out at us around every corner. By the time we entered an abandoned bedroom, my pulse was pounding in my ears and my body was trembling with a cocktail of fear and adrenaline.

They weren't messing around this year. This Haunted House was all kinds of intense.

Bant strolled to the bed in the middle of the barren room and sat down on the dirty mattress, leaning back on one elbow like he was posing in an ad for Calvin Klein. He was tempting fate with his laidback attitude. There was no way this room was as empty as it seemed.

A scream echoed from somewhere else in the house, making me shudder.

"Maybe it's intermission?" Bant offered, patting the mattress beside him. "Maybe they left this here to give us a break to get it on and regroup."

I crossed my arms over my chest, all of my senses on high alert. "Maybe your cocky attitude is going to be your undoing."

As if on cue, a crazed translucent skeleton creature reared up from a split down the middle of the mattress behind Bant. The grin was wiped from his face as the creature wrapped an arm around his shoulders, trying to pull him backwards on the bed.

"What the fuck!"

He bolted up, desperately trying to shake it off, and I couldn't help the laugh that burst out of me. He stumbled to my side with a shudder, the creature still snarling from the bed.

I wiped the tears from my eyes.

"Oh my God, that was terrifying and amazing all at the same time."

"Terrifying for you?" Bant said, ushering me out the door. "I'm the one who just got accosted by Gollum's possessed cousin."

He shuddered again, pulling me in front of him and gripping my shoulders as we shuffled out of the room.

"So, you're going to use me as a human shield now?"

"No, we need to stick together." He gave my shoulders the smallest squeeze. "I'm not letting you out of my reach. This place is spooky as fuck."

We moved into another room, this one with dark rock walls with what looked like thin veins of orange lava running through every inch of them.

"It's not so bad in here," Bant whispered.

I wanted to snap back that he had just screwed us by uttering those words, when a creature that had blended into the walls lunged for us.

I screamed and we hit the far wall in an effort to get away from it. Bant's arms wrapped around me and he curled his enormous body protectively over mine, as the creature with crazy sharp teeth and giant devil horns snarled at us.

Bant half-carried, half-shuffled me to the doorway at the

other end of the room, his warm body still wrapped around me like armor.

"I would have thought a she-devil like you would have welcomed those guys with open arms," Bant said, a smile in his voice.

My responding "shut up" made him chuckle.

"You must be seriously freaked out if you can't even deliver any of your usual snark."

I went to do just that when a chainsaw-wielding vampire jumped out at us. I let out a whimper and Bant shoved the thing back, one arm still wrapped protectively around me as he walked us to the next room.

"Okay, I admit it." My voice trembled in the dark. "I'm freaked out."

My heart was racing and no amount of steadying breaths was slowing it down. This was way scarier than last year and I wanted to get the hell out of here.

Where was the damn exit?

Instead of finding it, we turned a corner and faced another pitch-black space.

Bant's arms slid from my body as he came to stand beside me. I bit down on my whimper, fighting the urge to curl into him again.

"It's almost over." He slid his hand in mine in the dark, and I gripped it hard.

"How do you possibly know that?"

"I just do." He gave my hand a squeeze. "Follow me."

The darkness was totally overwhelming. I couldn't see my own fingers when I waved them in front of my face. How Bant knew where he was walking, I had no idea.

I tried to hide my panting breaths, embarrassed by my fear. I let Bant tow me into what was another hallway, a long one by the echo of our footsteps, walls caging us in on either side. It seemed totally unassuming, save for the darkness.

Which meant I should have known they'd save the worst for last.

I should have known the final hallway would be the stuff of nightmares.

Without warning invisible hands reached out through the darkness, what felt like hundreds of them, clawing at my hair, my face, my arms, my clothes.

A scream tore out of me and my hand slipped from Bant's to swipe at them, trying to shove them off.

"Oh my God! Stop!"

I screamed again, the hands clawing and pawing and shoving me. My shoulder bounced against the wall, only for more hands to paw at me from that side, making my skin crawl and my heart pound painfully in my chest.

"Bant!"

The hands just kept coming at me. When I was shoved into the wall again, I slid down it, curling into a ball on the floor. If I wasn't so terrified, I might have been embarrassed at cowering like a small child, but right now, I didn't care. I just wanted to get the hell out of here.

"Bant!" I screamed his name into my hands where they covered my face.

"Imogen?"

Footsteps sounded in the dark, his feet shuffling as he felt around in the darkness trying to find me. A moment later I was scooped up and held against his hard chest.

Hands still grabbed at us and I screamed at them to stop, my voice more hysterical than I'd ever heard it. Bant carried me down the hallway, pushing through a curtain into another dark room, only this one had some light cracking through a door with a glowing EXIT sign overhead.

Bant set me on my feet, holding me by the shoulders and peering at me, concern etched on his face. "Are you okay?"

I shook my head. "I can't breathe."

His hand slid from my shoulder to my chest, his warm palm against my shirt. "Holy shit, your heart is racing. Im, you need to calm down." He took my hand and placed it over his heart so I could feel the steadying rhythm. "Take deep breaths with me."

I nodded, trying to do what he said. But all I could think about were those hands all over me in the dark, clawing at me like they were going to tear me apart. I could still feel them in my hair and on my skin.

"They kept touching me," I said, eyes filling with tears as the adrenaline ebbed from my body. "I couldn't get them off, they just kept touching me."

I knew how shrill I sounded but I couldn't make it stop. The panic I'd felt in that blacked-out hallway was building inside me again, my breaths getting shorter, my chest starting to ache from the pressure.

"Imogen, look at me." Bant held my face in both hands, tilting my head so our eyes locked. "You need to calm down. It's over. Breathe with me."

I knew he was right, only I couldn't get the air in to make it happen.

So many hands. All over me.

My breathing shortened, my body wracking with shudders and I could focus on nothing else. I was in danger of a full-blown panic attack.

Without warning, Bant crowded my space, the heat of

him overwhelming me. His mouth closed over mine, his lips warm and soft and urgent.

My body jolted with surprise, rigid in his arms. Then without a thought, I kissed him back, letting go and allowing myself to be consumed by him.

The fear and tension slowly eased, my body slackening against him. The hand still pressed to his chest closed into a fist around his shirt, tugging him closer. My lips parted and his tongue swept into my mouth, brushing over mine in warm, distracting strokes. His hand trailed from my face, down my side, scorching a path to my waist. I let out a soft moan when his fingers closed over my hip, edging me closer until our bodies were pressed together.

Taking control, I nudged him backwards until his back hit the wall. He smiled against my mouth, his hold on me tightening. Everything else slipped away, the fear and panic replaced by Bant's hands on my body and his mouth on mine.

At some point my leg hitched at his waist in an effort to get closer and he held me behind the knee, grinding me against him.

Screams echoed in the dark hallway nearby and suddenly a group appeared in the room with us, rowdy and laughing. We broke the kiss but didn't pull away, our chests heaving as we stared at each other.

The group shot us curious looks as they made their way to the door, Bant and I shielding our eyes as natural light flooded the room.

Holy shit, I'd just made out with Bant.

He'd been trying to help me, but all that kiss had done was awaken parts of me I've been trying to bury this year, and made me feel things for Luke Bantempelli that I swore I'd never allow.

What was it I'd said only last week at the basketball court? I'd rather weld on a steel chastity belt than let Bant's tongue anywhere near me?

Well, shit.

In my defense, I had no idea what an insanely good kisser the guy was.

But then again, knowing all the magic ways to move your mouth was part of the job description for a campus playboy. There was no way he bedded as many girls as he did with a brillo pad tongue he didn't know how to use.

Bant dropped my knee, pulling me back to reality, and I stepped away, putting space between us.

"Thank you..." I avoided his eye. "For... um... helping me. I didn't expect to react that way."

He shrugged like it was nothing. "Always happy to help a girl in need."

Of course he was. He'd been helping needy girls all over campus for the past four years.

"I guess we should..." I motioned towards the door.

"I guess so."

We moved at the same time, but I stopped him with a hand to the chest.

He stared down at where our bodies touched, then back at me.

"While I'm grateful for your help in here... if you tell anyone about this, I'll lock you in that bedroom with Gollum's cousin and let him have his way with you."

Those baby blues sparked with amusement.

"Secret's safe with me, Sweets."

EIGHT

IMOGEN

I HOVERED outside the basketball locker room feeling like the kind of desperate super fan I definitely wasn't. Players slowly trickled out, some ignoring me completely, others giving me a once-over before strolling off.

"Imogen?" Davis stopped just outside the door, letting it slam behind him. "Never thought I'd see you hanging out in this hallway."

He glanced up and down it as if waiting for the punch-line to a joke. Or a hidden camera for some kind of TikTok prank.

"I'm waiting for someone."

He raised an eyebrow. "And who's that?"

I sighed. "Bantempelli."

"He's still inside." Davis motioned over his shoulder. "He's the only one left in there if you want to head in."

I hesitated. "Sure. Thanks D."

He started strolling down the hall. "Don't do anything I wouldn't do."

"That really doesn't leave much."

His chuckle echoed back to me. It was true though — Davis rivalled Bant for the biggest man whore on the team. He'd probably seen and done it all at this point.

Steeling myself, I hauled open the door to the locker room and was immediately hit with the overwhelming scent cocktail of socks, sweat, and man smell. The giant room was empty, lockers packed with uniforms, shoes, and gym bags. The door to the coach's office was closed, the space dark, and Bant was nowhere to be seen.

The sound of the shower running caught my attention and I edged in that direction, both concerned and a little curious about what might be about to assault my eyeballs.

When I rounded the corner, Bant was standing naked in one of the stalls about halfway down, the short, tiled wall covering all the bits that needed to be covered, leaving his glistening torso on display. His eyes were closed, water running through his dark blond hair and cascading over his toned shoulders.

Jesus. Why had I willingly walked in here?

The guy already had an ego the size of Texas, I didn't need to get caught ogling him and fueling it even further. He'd never let it go.

I turned on my heel to get the hell out when his voice echoed in the room. "Too late, you've already been busted watching me shower."

I swiveled slowly, grimacing at Bant's shit-eating grin at catching me out.

"Never pegged you for a peeping tom, you little deviant."

I planted my hands on my hips. "I wasn't peeping."

He squirted body wash into his hands, soaping up his chest and abs.

Oh, for god's sake. He knew exactly what he was doing.

I swallowed, forcing myself to keep my eyes on his face and ignoring the flare of *something* low in my stomach. "I came to talk to you."

He quirked a brow. "In the locker room?"

"Davis... he..." I threw my hands up in exasperation. "You know what? It doesn't matter."

I made a beeline for the doorway, losing my nerve. I hated putting myself out there and being vulnerable in any way. Bant never took anything seriously, which meant he was always guaranteed to make things harder than they needed to be.

"Hold up," he called after me. "You want to talk. So here I am, let's talk."

He stared back at me, daring me to stay.

I took a deep breath, squared my shoulders and moved further into the room. Not close enough to see anything I shouldn't, but close enough to lean against the wall of the stall beside his.

"I wanted to thank you for what you did in the Haunted House."

He studied me. "You thanked me at the time."

I nodded. "I know, I just... I thought about it and what you did... it was..."

The water raining down his impressive body was beyond distracting. And mixed with the memory of what had gone down between us in the Haunted House, it was near impossible to focus. It should be illegal for someone to look that good in the shower. I had to shove down the sudden urge to lick every inch of his incredible glistening chest. He belonged in some kind of commercial because, right now, I'd buy anything he was selling.

Silence hung between us, a knowing grin spreading across Bant's face at my blatant perusal. "Taking a mental picture for when you're alone later?"

I rolled my eyes, frustrated at my own idiocy and for feeding his already rampant ego. "Look, I just came to say thanks. So... thanks again."

He shook his head, turning his chest towards the spray. "No, you didn't."

I frowned, my stirring desire at his Adonis body instantly replaced with annoyance. "Yes, I did. I think I know why I came here."

He shook his head again and I wanted to throttle him, naked or not.

"You came here because you can't stop thinking about how hot my mouth was on yours, and you want to do it again."

He ran both hands through his wet hair, his toned arms flexing.

I swallowed.

What the hell was wrong with me?

Yes, he was hot as hell, but so were a lot of guys, and I wasn't swooning over the sight of them. It had been a while since I'd been with anyone, but my body was reacting to him like a nun who had just escaped a lifetime of silent solitude at the convent.

"I don't know what you're talking about..."

He huffed a laugh. "You want to thank me? Send me a text. Pass a message through Monty. Snap me. You didn't need to wait outside the locker room and then invite yourself in while I showered just to tell me that, and we both know it."

I stared back at him, my jaw tightening. "You're acting like I'm some basketball groupie desperate for your dick."

He chuckled, watching me as his soaping hands dipped below the wall and out of view. "You're no basketball bunny. Desperate for the D though?" He gave me a loaded look that implied he knew exactly what I'd been thinking.

His unfettered arrogance riled every last shred of righteous indignation in me.

"It's amazing you're not exhausted at the end of every day after dragging that monster ego of yours around with you."

His grin widened. "It's not the only monstrous thing I'm carrying around all day."

I rolled my eyes. "Down boy. I'm not interested."

Only... that might've been a lie. I was a living breathing person with a pulse. A small part of me was definitely interested. And maybe he was right, maybe I had wanted to see him again after our toe-curling kiss in the Haunted House. My psych professors would assess this as a case of heightened emotions brought on by a fear-inducing situation. All I knew was I'd locked lips with plenty of guys since coming to Pierson and not one of them had made my body spark like Bant had. I couldn't help but wonder if it was a once-off or if it would happen again if I let him near my mouth.

Yet, my pride wouldn't let me admit that to his face.

"Who are you trying to convince?" Bant challenged. "Me or yourself?"

I crossed my arms over my chest, trying to appear more defiant than I felt. "I don't need to convince anyone of anything."

Those blue eyes zeroed in on me, making my stomach twist in the best way.

"Well, you wanted to thank me, I can think of a couple

of ways we can make that happen. Why don't you climb in here with me, and I'll talk you through them?"

He motioned to the shower, and I stared back at him, my mouth opening and closing.

"I'm not getting in the shower with you."

He shrugged. "Why not? You just admitted you want to feel my mouth on yours again. So let's get wet, Im."

"I never admitted to anything. If you want to believe your own spin, go ahead, playboy."

He gave me a knowing smile. "All you have to do is take a step and we won't be talking anymore."

It was a lie. It would take at least three steps around the stall wall for me to be in the shower with him, but clearly he didn't care about semantics. And honestly, neither did I. A huge part of me was dying to take a step and see exactly what would happen. Was he all talk or would he deliver on everything he'd just taunted me with?

Only my stubbornness kept my feet firmly planted.

I swallowed hard, trying to force my body to see logic. We'd already crossed the line by kissing, getting any more involved with a guy like Luke Bantempelli, no matter how hot his mouth was, would only end badly for me. He was the furthest thing from a one-woman kind of guy, which meant he was exactly the type I should be staying far away from. There was no way I could trust a guy like him when he was surrounded by girls dying for a piece of him and he regularly partook without a second thought. If the girls of Pierson U were a buffet, Bant was a repeat customer, sampling anything and everything they had to offer. If I had any kind of self preservation, there was no way I'd willingly open myself up to the kind of heartbreak that went hand in hand with getting involved with a womanizer like Bant. Stella and Monty had both lived with him last year, Monty still did. I'd heard the stories about how his bed was rarely cold for more than a few nights at a time.

Only... I couldn't stop thinking about that damn kiss.

And his glistening torso was beyond tempting.

"Come on, Im. Get out of that head of yours and just take a step. You know you want to."

"Don't presume you know anything about me," I cut back.

The sound of the shower was the only noise in the room as we stared at each other, the tension rising between us. He watched my every move with keen eyes, silently goading me to take a step.

It took everything I had to swallow my pride and inch towards the stall.

It was all the permission he needed, reaching out and tugging me around the wall and into the shower with him.

Our bodies instantly crushed together and water cascaded over my clothes.

His face split in a dazzling smile that made my heart stutter, and he slid his arms around me. "I knew you wanted me."

I prayed he couldn't hear my heart pounding in my chest at the feel of him against me.

"Pretty sure it's you who wants me, playboy." My hands glided up over his slick pecs and fastened around his neck. "Now shut up and deliver."

His eyes sparked as his mouth descended on mine, his hands moving to palm my ass through the now-soaked clothes clinging to my body.

This kiss was just as hot as the first, the stroke of his tongue making my knees weak. It was no surprise he'd never had a complaint from the girls who chose to hook up with him.

I ran my hands through his wet hair, just knowing he was naked even when I was fully clothed had me all kinds of turned on. His hands dipped under the hem of my shirt, gliding up my back to unhook my bra. His fingers trailed over my ribcage, our mouths never breaking contact. My breath hitched when his fingertips brushed against the underside of my breast, my body craving more.

Then a stern voice sliced through the moment.

"Bantempelli, what the hell are you doing?"

On a reflex, I hit the deck, dropping to the floor of the shower stall and finding myself face to face with Bant's hard length.

"Oh my fucking god," I muttered, both at being caught out and at the sheer size of the beast that was about to poke me in the eye.

He actually had sex with that thing? It was a fucking anaconda.

My thighs clenched just thinking about how I'd ever fit that inside me.

Not that I wanted to.

It was bad enough we'd made out twice now and been busted by his coach. Sex with Bant was absolutely, positively *not* on the table.

"I catch you pulling this in my locker room again, and I'll bench you, understood?"

Bant cleared his throat, his hands coming to cover his junk and saving me from a slap in the face. "You got it, Coach."

"And you better have some dry clothes for that girl. I don't want her walking out of here drenched and dripping everywhere."

Bant tried to hold back his snort at the double meaning to his coach's words, and I punched him in the thigh.

He winced, chuckling. "Sure thing, Coach."

There was a shuffling of footsteps, then the slamming of a door and the pounding of the shower was the only noise in the room again.

I covered my face in my hands. "Oh my god, I can't believe that just happened."

Bant's laugh echoed through the room. His hands closed around my arms, gently hauling me to my feet. "It's nothing he hasn't seen before."

I pulled a face. "Wow, real smooth. Way to make a girl feel special."

He looked momentarily stricken. "No, that's... not from me! I'm pretty sure Van and Stella got it on in here last year. And I know Davis sneaks girls in here all the time when there are too many people back at the house."

"Whatever you say, playboy."

He turned off the shower with one hand, then reached for his towel, wrapping it around my shoulders.

"You know..." he said, using the towel to tug me closer. "I never thought I'd have you dropping to your knees so soon."

I scowled, punching him in the pec and almost injuring my hand in the process.

"You better not tell..." I started, but he pressed a finger to my lips to stop me.

"I know, I know, I better not tell anyone about this or you'll feed my balls through a wood chipper. Like I said before, the secret is safe with me, Sweets."

NINE

IMOGEN

...

BANT: Noticed you turned up to the game in Hooker's jersey tonight. Cute. Was that just to piss me off or...?

IMOGEN: No, it was to show my team spirit. Go PU!

IMOGEN: Pissing you off was just an added bonus.

BANT: Sorry to break your heart, Sweets, but it didn't work. I've told you before, I'm more interested in how to get you out of my jersey than in it.

IMOGEN: Never going to happen.

I TRIED NOT to stare at Bant across the packed room and appear totally unaffected as yet another girl took the marker from his hand and signed his body, this time just above his right pec. So far, he'd spent the entire party shirtless, an endless parade of girls approaching him to sign their names on his skin as part of some inane basketball tradition they apparently did every year.

What exactly did girls signing your skin have to do with basketball?

Whatever it was, Bant was relishing every second of it.

I, on the other hand, couldn't stand it. And I couldn't stand that I couldn't stand it because when it came to Luke Bantempelli, I wanted to feel absolutely nothing.

Bant was throwing himself into the task with gusto, his eyes landing on me every now and then as he held still so yet another girl could brand him.

Ugh. I refuse to let him get under my skin.

Clearly this was payback for wearing Hooker's jersey to the game, even though he'd been adamant in his text that he didn't care. But what did he expect from me? He wasn't my boyfriend, we were barely even hooking up. We'd kissed twice. I wasn't about to walk around with his name on my back like some devoted basketball girlfriend. Besides, there had been plenty of girls in the stadium tonight who'd had his name emblazoned on their backs. He didn't need me.

But watching him now, making his way through the party, random girls stopping him every few minutes to sign their names or phone numbers or life savings over to him via his abs was making my pulse pound behind my eyes, the stirrings of a headache coming on.

I needed to get a grip. What did it matter if Bant wanted to offer his body to every girl on campus? It had nothing to do with me. And it *meant* nothing to me.

So why the hell was I standing here watching it happen like some kind of sad fangirl?

"Parties are supposed to be fun, you know," Monty said, appearing at my side and leaning against the kitchen counter next to me.

I glanced at her. "I am having fun."

"Really? Because that permanent scowl on your face says otherwise." She glanced around the room. "Who's ruining your night? You want me to have them beaten up or kicked out?"

I laughed. Pretty sure she couldn't get Bant kicked out of his own house. Nor was I ever going to admit that I'd been risking permanent wrinkles by scowling over him.

So what if he had a monster dick and was an incredible kisser? That was no reason to let my sudden lust run away with me. He also had a giant ego and was a permanent pain in my ass.

Only... when I was alone in bed at night, I couldn't stop picturing that monster dick that had almost slapped me across the face. I knew it would be a better ride than any toy I'd ever tried.

"Maybe you need to get laid?" Monty suggested, downing her drink. "It's been a while since Bobby."

I cringed at the reminder of my ex-boyfriend. He was a jerk, and I'd successfully erased him from my life the moment he'd cheated on me. I refused to be hurt by someone who was such a deceitful asshole. And yet, here I was letting the hurt he'd caused dictate my life.

Was Monty right? Would a good old-fashioned boning be the perfect antidote to clear out the ghosts of boyfriends' past and move on?

There would be no need for feelings or follow up or any of the other annoying things that went along with getting properly involved with someone. What I needed was an hour of sweaty sex and then a quick goodbye.

It was a good thing I knew a guy who could play that role perfectly.

The fact it meant the basketball groupies wouldn't be

able to paw at him for the rest of the night was just an added bonus. It didn't mean I was jealous. And it *definitely* didn't mean I was into him.

I just wanted to get laid.

Discarding my drink on the counter behind me, I made my way through the party, edging around the gathered group of drooling girls.

It was time to see if his trouser snake was worth more than a slap in the face.

TEN

BANT

IMOGEN APPEARED BEFORE ME, planting a hand to my chest and shoving me back. I let myself stumble until my back hit the wall, a grin spreading across my face.

If she wanted to man-handle me, I was damn well going to let her. I didn't care what she did if it meant her hands were on me. I'd had plenty of girls pawing at me tonight while they signed my skin; it should have been enjoyable, but there was only one girl I actually wanted... and now here she was.

"Let's go to your room."

I stilled, my brow creasing in a frown. "I must have had way more to drink tonight than I thought, because it sounded like you just demanded to go to my room."

She crossed her arms over her chest, blocking the view of her luscious tits. "That's what I said."

I stared back at her, paralyzed with indecision. Was this some kind of girl test? Was I supposed to say no and prove I liked her for more than just sex? Or was she really telling me she wanted to get it on right now?

Her brow pinched and she looked pissed. "Did you take a ball to the head this week? Are we going to your room or not?"

A laugh burst out of me. "You're not bullshitting me right now?"

"No, I'm not bullshitting you. But the longer you make me stand here, the more I want to change my mind."

I took her hand before she could utter another word, towing her through the party and steamrolling anyone who got in my way. When we reached the stairs I motioned for her to go first, mostly so I could stare at her ass in her dress as she climbed.

We made it my room, and she ushered me in like she owned the place, shutting the door behind me.

Hell no, this is my damn house.

Imogen liked to think she was in charge, but not this time.

I crowded her from behind, pinning her front against the inside of my bedroom door. "Is this what you were hoping for when we came up here?"

"Yes."

The breathy tone to her voice made my dick jerk against my zipper.

She looked at me over her shoulder, and I leaned around, closing my mouth over hers. She opened for me, our tongues colliding in a way that made me groan and grind against her.

I slid my hands over her hips and down her thighs to dip beneath her dress. I slid her underwear down her smooth thighs and she stepped out of them, gasping when my fingers trailed back up over her slick center, her ass pushing back against my hard cock still trapped in my jeans.

"Bant..."

Her head fell back against my shoulder, her hands splayed on the door, as I worked my fingers over her.

I increased the pace and her body vibrated with pleasure, her fingers tensing against the door so hard her knuckles whitened.

"Oh my God... who knew you were so good with your hands?"

I smirked, my mouth at her ear. "You could have been enjoying the pleasure a long time ago if you weren't so intent on hating me."

She let out a frustrated growl, and I moved my fingers faster. Whatever snappy retort she'd been about to utter died on her lips.

"Oh fuck, I'm going to..."

Fuck, that was fast. And damn if my ego didn't love it.

Her whole body tightened, pressing back against mine. Her head tipped back against my shoulder and she let out a moan, pleasure ripping through her. I stroked her through her come down, until she gripped my wrist, stilling me.

When I withdrew my hand, she glanced at me over her shoulder and her hand slipped between us, rubbing over my cock in my jeans. She moved to turn around, but I gripped her waist, holding her in place.

"You can take care of that next time."

She scowled at me. "Next time? There's not going to be a next time. This is a one-time deal, playboy."

I slid her dress up over her phenomenal ass. "Whatever you say, Sweets."

I never thought she'd give me even one shot at having her, so I wasn't going to argue now. I didn't know what I'd done to suddenly deserve access to her incredible body, and I was going to relish every second she was allowing me to have my hands on her.

I unzipped at lightning speed, my cock springing free, and I reached for a condom from the dresser by the door.

She smirked back at me. "Someone's keen to get inside."

"You have no fucking idea."

She thrust her ass towards me, getting into position and my fingers tightened on her waist.

"Look at you, getting ready for me like a good girl."

She let out a half growl, half whimper at the praise, and I slid the tip of my dick along her fold, both of us groaning with need at the contact. Without another word, I thrust inside her, the moan she let out as I filled her almost enough to make me come on the spot.

I pulled back, fingers tightening at her hips to steady us both as I slid inside her again.

"Yes, Bant, oh my god..."

Her ass came back to meet every thrust, sending me deeper each time, and she moaned my name over and over.

"Fuck yeah, I love the way you say my name like that."

She threw a look at me over her shoulder and it was the hottest thing I'd ever fucking witnessed.

"Don't let it go to your head, I still can't stand you."

"Is that why you're letting me fuck you right now? Because you can't stand me?"

I tunnelled in deep, practically seeing stars at how good she felt.

She scowled, pushing back off the door and turning so I stumbled back a step and slid out of her.

What the...

I reached for her, my cock desperate to be buried deep

inside her again, but she put a firm hand to my chest, stopping me.

"Let's get one thing straight. I'm letting you fuck me because I'm horny, and I know you're good at it. That's it."

I reached for her. "Good enough for me, boss."

Only Imogen would stop mid-fuck to grill me.

And yet, I relished every second of that fire in her eyes. If she kept this up, she was in danger of making me want her more than I already did. All she needed to do was call me a jackass while I was balls deep in her, and I'd be shooting my load in under a minute.

"Stop looking at me with pathetic puppy dog eyes and rail me like you mean it."

Fuck me.

Faster than she could blink, I gripped the back of her head and slammed my mouth over hers, our tongues tangling in a hot, open-mouthed kiss. I pinned her to the door, lifting her legs out from under her and thrusting into her.

"This good enough for you, Sweets?"

She bit her lip and gripped my shoulders, nodding. I pistoned my hips, sliding in and out of her, both of us panting hard in an instant. She was so damn tight, I was ready to come from one thrust.

"Oh shit, oh shit, oh shit..." she moaned, clawing at the door above her head.

I loved how vocal she was, her words turning me to steel inside her.

We moved together, our slick bodies gliding over each other until we were both teetering on the edge.

"Fuck, baby, you feel so good."

"Don't call me that," she panted, her eyes shut tight with pleasure, her head thrown back.

I pummelled into her faster, liquid heat pooling at the base of my spine.

There was no way I could come before she did. She'd never let me forget it. But there was nothing I could do, she felt way too damn good. Not even thoughts of Hooker's hairy ass were going to pull me from the moment and stop me exploding inside her.

But I didn't need to worry about holding back. The next second Imogen's arms tightened around my shoulders in a vice grip. She buried her face at my throat, her walls tightening around my cock as she clung to me. Then she tipped her head back and moaned my name, making me come hard at the sound, and the feel of my cock buried deep inside her.

Eventually we stilled, holding onto each other, the room suddenly quiet save for our breathless pants.

Imogen's legs loosened at my waist, and I slid free, setting her down.

"Thanks, that was great," she said, patting my shoulder like I was an obedient pet. Then she turned to leave.

That's not fucking happening.

I gripped the back of her neck, tugging her back to me, and our mouths collided again. She let out a small noise of surprise, but opened for me, my tongue sweeping into her mouth.

When we broke apart, I couldn't help my smirk at her stunned expression.

"It was fucking life changing and you know it."

ELEVEN

BANT

...

BANT: Jericho's jersey this time? Really? He's giving me endless shit over it.

IMOGEN: What can I say, I like the number twelve

BANT: What exactly do you like about it?

IMOGEN: That it's not yours and that drives you crazy 😇

"WHAT'S GOING on with you? You've been lost in that head of yours all afternoon," Raven said, pulling a box of potatoes from the back of the truck we were unloading outside the kitchens at the shelter.

I shrugged, stacking the box I was holding on top of the others. "Girl trouble, I guess."

"A stud like you?" Her tone was teasing.

I chuckled. "I wouldn't usually let myself get caught up in feelings and all that emotional junk, but..."

Raven watched me, her smile amused. "This one is different?"

"Yeah, she is. She doesn't let me get away with my usual bullshit. I never know what the hell she's going to do one minute to the next."

I hauled another box of vegetables from the back of the truck, adding it to the growing pile inside the kitchen.

"I like the sound of her," Raven said, doing the same. "So, what exactly is the problem then?"

I sighed, running a hand through my hair while I thought about it.

"I've been trying to hook up with this girl since we met."

Raven shot me a look. "Talk about playing the long game. I didn't think you college boys had attention spans that long when it came to women."

I raised a brow. "This one is different, remember?"

"Evidently."

I hauled another box from the back of the truck. "We finally hooked up at a party."

Raven frowned. "And... it wasn't any good?"

"No, it was fucking phenomenal."

"Then I fail to see the problem..."

"I haven't heard from her since. She hasn't replied to anything."

It was true. Since our texts after the team's latest game where Imogen had shown up in Jeri's jersey, I hadn't heard a word out of her. The girl was a master at playing it cool. Either that or she genuinely wasn't interested in sleeping with me again. But the way she'd been moaning against my fingers and while riding my dick, I was pretty confident it wasn't the sex that had her running.

A laugh burst out of Raven. "Never thought I'd see the day a girl ghosted you. Not with those cheekbones and baby blues. I'm sure it's usually the other way around, right?"

I levelled her with a flat stare. "I don't ghost girls."

"Oh, please. Ghosting is standard practice with you kids now, isn't it? You're all too scared to tell someone to their face you're not interested."

"Well, I'm interested in this one. I refuse to accept that I'm being fucking ghosted."

Raven stopped, placing her hands on her hips. "So instead of whining to me about it, why don't you find out why she's gone quiet?"

Part of me already knew why.

Imogen didn't let anyone get close to her, that much was clear from the past two years we'd spent going at each other. Only now that I'd had a taste of her, I didn't want to be like every other dude she'd sidelined. Yes, I wanted to sleep with her again, but it was more than that. Imogen was all hard edges and sass and I loved every second of it. Who wanted to be with a girl who actually liked you when you could have someone tell you they can't stand you while you pounded them from behind? No other girl was going to cut it when I'd had a taste of pure fire personified.

Hauling the last three boxes from the back of the truck, I dropped them inside the kitchen.

"Mind if I head out a little early, Raven?"

She gave me a knowing smile. "Sure thing, kid. Good luck convincing her not to ghost your ass."

I JUMPED IN MY CAR, pulling out my phone to text Monty. Pretty sure she and Imogen did yoga together on campus on Wednesdays.

BANT: *Yo, you at yoga RN?*

MONTY: *No, Dad. I'm with my writing group.*

BANT: *Yoga's in the Drysdale rec room, right?*

MONTY: *Yeah, why?*

I didn't bother replying, starting my car and heading across campus. I made it to the Drysdale building, slipping into the rec room near the front.

There were about twelve people in the class, eleven girls and one guy, all contorting in the same pretzel-looking position on the floor. The cute redheaded instructor gave me a serene smile as I took a seat on the bench at the back of the room.

"Now transition from that position to work through your flow," she said, walking on silent feet in my direction.

Everyone followed her instructions, bending and dipping through their movements.

"Are you interested in trying some yoga?" the redhead asked in a quiet, whispy voice.

I gave her a dazzling smile. "I'm always up for new things. But in this case, I'm just waiting for a friend. I promise you won't hear a peep out of me."

She nodded, giving me a once over that was an all-too common occurrence from the girls on campus, before returning to the front of the room. She could look all she wanted, but unless she suddenly morphed into a five-foot-seven dark-haired ice queen with a mouth on her, I wasn't interested.

The class wrapped up a couple of minutes later and Imogen got to her feet in the front row. She turned to roll up her mat, placing it in the corner with the others, stopping short when she spotted me at the back of the room.

She headed for her stuff, seemingly content to ignore me.

"Sweaty suits you," I said, making my way over and leaning against the wall beside her. "Be better if I was the one who'd gotten you that way though."

She took a sip of her water bottle, ignoring my suggestion. "What are you doing here? Decided a yoga babe would be a nice bendy addition to your bedroom roster?"

I fought a smile. "I decided that the second I started pursuing you."

She ignored me, pulling a sweatshirt over her tight little crop top and covering up her amazing rack.

"You haven't been replying to my texts."

"So, you thought you'd stalk me at yoga?"

"I don't know if I'd call turning up one time stalking. But if that's a kink of yours, I'll role play it out with you, Sweets."

"Hard pass." She turned to me, hands on both her hips. "Seriously, what are you doing here?"

I crossed my arms over my chest, shoulder still pressed to the wall like I wasn't at all squirming under her scrutiny. Despite not replying to my messages, I thought maybe she'd at least be happy to see me. But the girl was frostier than a snow cone, and my ego was taking an uncharacteristic hit.

"I came to talk to you."

"About?"

"How you should go out with me."

She stared at me, then let out a laugh. "Absolutely no way."

I tried not to appear as affronted as I felt at the instant rejection. Imogen was prickly, she made no secret of that. But I thought given the smoking hot sex we'd had that she'd at least consider the possibility of dinner with me before tossing the idea aside.

"Care to tell me why you're so dead against the idea?"

"Because I don't date campus playboys."

I grinned. "Good thing I'm not one, then."

"Right, all those women in your bed the past few years just stumbled in there by accident? Got lost on their way to the library?"

I went to dispute her, but in the absolute worst timing possible one of the girls from the class strolled by on her way out, shooting me a flirty smile.

"Hi Bant."

I gave her a nod and a tight smile in return, groaning internally at just how badly that one small greeting was going to screw me over with the spandex-clad cactus in front of me.

"And... I'm out," Imogen said, stepping around me and heading for the door.

I followed her into the night air, passing the girl that had just inadvertently tanked my attempts at getting Imogen to spend time with me.

Imogen was a tough one to crack. But the caustic way she made me work for her attention was one of the things that intrigued me about her. Maybe I was a masochist.

"Wait just a sec, that's not my fault," I said, motioning over my shoulder at the girl walking away. I tried to fight my smile. I really did. "I can't help it if Yoga Girl wants to say hi to me. She's probably seen me play and knows what a stud I am on the court."

Imogen was halfway down the path outside the building when she rounded on me, face pinched with aggravation, and I mentally congratulated myself on riling her enough to talk to me.

"You're really full of yourself, you know that?"

I nodded, grinning.

I knew it. She knew it. Anyone who walked within three feet of me knew it. It was all part of my charm, and while Imogen might claim to hate it, the way her eyes sparked with fire when we went at each other told me that was a lie.

She crossed her arms over her chest, her expression filled with disdain. I wanted to tug her into my arms and kiss the hell out of her.

"Well, it's not hot."

"You thought it was hot over the weekend when *you* were full of me."

She was momentarily outraged, and I couldn't stop the laugh that burst out of me at the sight.

"I hate you," she tried, but the smile playing at the corners of her mouth didn't really sell it.

"You want me."

I ignored her scoff and stepped closer, relishing the victory when she didn't move away.

"You're delusional," she offered.

"And you're hot when you're mad."

"Well, in that case, I must look like a supermodel to you whenever you're anywhere near me."

I hooked a finger in the pocket of her leggings, tugging her closer. "I've missed that mouth of yours..."

Before she could reply, I slid a hand along her jaw and kissed her. She stilled, momentarily surprised, then she slowly leaned into it, her body relaxing against mine.

Her hands trailed up my chest and when she kissed me back and pressed her hips to mine, I wanted to groan into her mouth.

"Go out with me," I said when we eventually broke apart.

She rolled her eyes. "No."

"Why not?"

"Because I don't want to."

"That kiss says you do."

"That kiss says I want to get laid. Nothing else."

I grinned. "I can take care of that too."

She slipped from my hold, slowly backing away down the path.

"Nice try, playboy, but dating isn't going to happen for us. Play your cards right though, and I might consider letting you in my pants again."

She turned and strolled away, my eyes dropping to her ass in her yoga pants that fit her like a second skin.

Fuck, I want her moaning my name again so badly.

At least she was talking to me.

At this point, I'd take whatever she was willing to give me.

TWELVE

IMOGEN

"THIS MOVIE IS SCARY AS SHIT," Hooker said from where he was sprawled on the floor hugging a cushion.

Monty, Stella and I were crashing the guys' movie night at the basketball house. We'd planned to go to dinner and instead found ourselves cooking for everyone and agreeing to watch a horror movie.

"It's tame," Davis said, throwing a handful of popcorn at his teammate. "You're just a wimp, Hooker."

"Leave him alone." Stella slid down in her spot beside me on the couch. "I'm kind of scared."

Bant shifted in the armchair to my right and I forced my eyes to stay trained on the screen. I'd been hyper-aware of him from the moment he'd strolled into the kitchen earlier tonight when we'd been cooking, but there was no way I'd let him know it.

He'd said hi when I'd arrived, giving me the nod like he hadn't turned up at my yoga class last night and kissed me stupid while begging for a date. I'd asked him to keep whatever was or wasn't happening between us a secret and so far he'd held up his end of the deal. Had it really only been last week that I'd been moaning his name while he nailed me against his bedroom door?

That night had delivered the most aggressive orgasm any guy had ever pulled from me. And just that one kiss yesterday had me so turned on and worked up, I'd gone home and taken care of myself in the shower. If I had my way, he and I would be going at it in his room right now.

But Bant being Bant went and ruined it all with his cocky bullshit.

He'd taken it upon himself to torture me all through dinner, grilling me on what I'd been up to lately and if I was seeing anyone, all in front of our friends whose attention bounced between us like they were watching a champion tennis match. When I'd sniped at him about minding his own business, he suggested getting laid more regularly might improve my surly personality. His self-satisfied smirk at my outrage had me sitting on my hands to stop myself from stabbing my fork into his thigh under the table.

His arrogance was insufferable and the surest way to piss him off in return was to starve his ego of attention.

So, that's what I was determined to do.

Only... despite my best intentions, the memory of his dick was just too damn strong. I'd spent most of the movie thinking up ways we could get naked again without our friends noticing. Then kick myself for daydreaming about getting it on with Luke Bantempelli when he was such an insufferable ass.

Maybe I should ask one of my professors for a psych eval...

So what if he was an incredible lay? So were a lot of guys. I could find another one.

Good luck finding one who can make you come that hard.

I shoved the thought aside, crossing my arms over my chest, practically huffing at my own ridiculousness. It was one orgasm. I wasn't going to let myself obsess over him just because he'd proven he could get me off in about forty seconds flat.

"You okay over there?" Monty whispered, eyeing me.

I plastered on a smile. "Never better."

Bant pushed to his feet. "I'm getting a drink. Don't bother pausing the movie, I think I can keep up."

I refused to let my gaze trail him out of the room. I didn't care what he did. Not one bit.

Only... when ten minutes passed and he hadn't come back, I found I did care.

Where the hell is he?

It really didn't take that long to pour a drink.

I slid to my feet. "I need the bathroom."

Monty and Stella both nodded, their attention wholly focused on the screen as I slipped from the room and made my way to the kitchen to find Bant leaning into the open fridge, assessing the contents.

"The options are slim but pick your poison, Im. What are you in the mood for?"

The cocky bastard didn't even turn around, he'd been that sure I'd follow him. The thought was so irritating I almost didn't utter the words I desperately wanted to.

But there was no reason for me to miss the opportunity for another incredible experience with his dick, just because the guy attached to it had an ego the size of Saturn.

"I'm in the mood for sex."

The fridge door slammed and Bant swivelled, his face a picture of surprise. "Come again?"

A smile spread across my face. "Exactly."

I rounded the counter, trailing a hand along the cool surface until I reached the door to the laundry room. I paused, glancing at him over my shoulder. "Coming to show me a good time or do I need to do it myself?"

He practically tripped over his own feet in his rush to follow me, flinging the door shut behind us and scooping my legs out from under me. He deposited me on top of the washing machine, hand tangling in my hair and pulling my mouth to his. His mouth was warm and eager, his kiss making my whole body sing like a top forty hit.

His hands slid up my thighs. "I must have been a very good boy to earn myself round two."

I rolled my eyes, leaning back and lifting my hips so he could slide down my jeans.

"You've been a pain in my ass and you know it. So don't make me question this, just get on with it."

"I'll get on with it any time you want, Sweets. All you have to do is ask."

I gripped his hair, pulling his head back, and a giant grin spread across his irritatingly handsome face.

"How many times have I told you not to call me that?"

"Not enough, apparently."

I scowled, letting go, and his grin widened.

"Fuck, you're hot when you're mad."

"You've mentioned that once or twice."

Annoyance and desire were twin flares inside me, and I tugged him closer, kissing him hard, our tongues clashing in a hot mess.

"You have five minutes to get this done and get me off

before someone gets suspicious and comes looking for us, so you might want to pull out your best work, playboy."

He didn't hesitate, his fingers sliding between my legs and stroking over my core. I tipped my head back and sighed, satisfied that he was finally giving me exactly what I wanted.

He really was a master with his fingers. Not that I'd ever tell him that. I'm sure every girl that had come before me had lavished him with praise in the bedroom, he didn't need me to stroke his ego while I stroked his package.

His other hand pulled my loose V-neck t-shirt aside, making short work of my lace bralette to expose my breast.

"Your tits are the most perfect set I've ever held. I dream about them."

He sucked my nipple into his mouth, the combination of his tongue and his fingers making my breath hitch as pleasure pulsed through me.

I reached for the waistband of his basketball shorts, slipping my hand inside and closing around his hardened shaft. I pumped him in my hand and he groaned against my breast.

"Four minutes," I reminded him and his hand disappeared from between my legs to drop his shorts to the floor.

"Shit..." He looked contrite. "I don't have any protection."

I shoved him back, reaching for my jeans around my ankles and pulling a condom from the back pocket.

His eyebrows shot up. "Seems I made a killer impression during round one if someone came to a girls' dinner this prepared. Hoping you'd get the chance to sneak away so I could fuck you?"

I rolled my eyes. "Three damn minutes, Bant. Do you

want to chat like sorority sisters or do you want to get each other off?"

He tore the rubber open, rolling it on faster than I'd ever seen him move. Gripping my ass, he slid me to the edge of the washing machine.

"Hold on tight, Sweets."

He thrust inside me, slamming himself to the hilt. I cried out at the sudden pressure and intense pleasure that shot through me, and he clapped a hand over my mouth.

"That was loud enough for the whole damn street to hear you. If you don't want our friends to know how good I am at this, then you need to keep a lid on it."

I bit my lip and this time when he pulled out, he covered my mouth with his, swallowing my moan as he thrust in deep.

Reaching behind me, he turned the dial on the machine and it vibrated beneath me, the sensation heightening the pleasure building inside me.

"To cover the insanely hot sounds you're making." He smirked. "And get you off faster."

He gripped my waist, increasing his punishing pace until we were both panting with need, the machine rumbling away.

Holy shit, it feels amazing.

His hands on me, his mouth on me, him buried deep inside me. It had never been this good with anyone, not even Bobby. And that boy had been bonafide dicksand for me. Right up until I'd found out I wasn't the only one he was giving his dick to.

"Talk to me, Im," Bant muttered, his hand sliding over my throat to tangle in my hair. "Tell me how much you want it, tell me how good it feels."

As much as I was loathe to give in to anything he

demanded, there was no denying what an incredible lay he was.

He's had plenty of practice.

I pushed the thought aside. If I didn't want to be judged for the number of people I'd slept with, I couldn't go doing it to him.

"It feels... so... good," I panted through his thrusts. "Best... I've ever... had."

His eyes flared with heat, his grip on me tightening and he pumped harder.

"Yeah?"

"Yes!"

The machine kicked up a notch, rumbling faster beneath me and, matched with Bant's cock filling me, it took about three-point-eight seconds before my core tightened and pleasure tore through my body. Bant covered my mouth with his hand to stifle my cries, and I bit down on his finger. He came hard at the same time, shuddering against me.

We both panted through the come down, his fingers tightening and releasing at my waist as he worked to catch his breath.

"Holy fuck, that was even better than last time."

I reached around behind me, shutting off the machine. "Who knew the playboy actually knows how to play?"

"Please, I have so many moves and you love every single one."

He pulled out, stripping off the condom and tucking his dick back in his shorts, before sliding my jeans back up my legs.

He stilled, brushing my hair back from my face, those baby blues that made so many girls across campus swoon turning serious.

"Go out with me, Im."

I resisted the urge to roll my eyes again as I gently pushed him aside and jumped down from the machine. "You tried this already, the answer is no."

I couldn't understand why he was pushing this. He and I together didn't work together, unless we were naked. The ghost of my orgasm still shivering through me was hard proof of that. But in an exclusive, emotional committed relationship? We'd be a disaster.

He shot me a rueful look as I buttoned my jeans, and I leaned in to give him a chaste peck on the lips.

"Thanks for the quickie. Now you've got two memories of me to beat off to when you're lonely."

His responding chuckle followed me out the door.

THIRTEEN

BANT

...

BANT: Li's jersey tonight. I'm so happy for him.

IMOGEN: Me too. He really seemed to appreciate the gesture.

BANT: I've got a few gestures I can think of that I'd appreciate from you *eggplant emoji*

IMOGEN: Jesus Bant, do you ever take a day off from trying to get into someone's pants?

BANT: Not when the pants in question are yours, Sweets.

I PICKED up a pebble on the ground at my feet, pitching it at what I was pretty sure was Imogen's window. It ricocheted off the glass, flinging back to hit me in the face.

"Ow, goddamn it!"

I clutched my eye. Throwing rocks while drunk wasn't my best move, but obviously I wasn't thinking clearly.

Didn't mean I was going to stop though.

I scooped up another pebble, stumbling on my feet a little and throwing my hands out to right myself.

"Woah, you okay, dude?" I asked the oak tree beside me.

When it didn't reply, I tossed another stone. It pinged off the glass this time and the light of a phone screen lit up the room inside a moment later. A black shadow moved behind the window, then it slid open and Imogen poked her head out.

"Bant, what the hell are you doing?" she hissed into the dark.

Words failed me, I was too mesmerised by the sight of all the smooth skin she was showing off in the tight, thin-strap black tank top she was wearing.

Fuck, she was incredible.

Everything about her made my chest ache or my dick twitch. Sometimes both.

"I was partying with my teammates, but I wanted to see you."

She glanced at the phone in her hand. "It's one am."

I shrugged. "The urge to see you doesn't really run on a clock for me, Sweets. It happens when it happens."

She was on the second floor, it was dark, and I'd downed way too many beers with the boys tonight, but I was pretty sure she rolled her eyes at me.

"Maybe next time call or text?"

I squinted at her. "Would you have answered?"

"No, probably not."

I spread my hands wide, vindicated. "Well, then, here I am in the flesh. So, Rapunzel, you going to let me up so I can make all your dreams come true?"

She leaned her elbows on the window frame like she was in no rush to let me in. "It's funny because I don't remember dreaming about being drooled on by a drunken idiot."

"Yeah, call me names. I love it when you talk dirty to me."

I squinted up at her and was pretty sure she was trying to fight a smile. I'd consider that a victory.

"You know you want to let me up." I cupped a hand to my mouth, stage-whispering up at her. "I'll even let you see my dick, I know how much you love it."

She pulled a face. "Great to know your ego only gets worse when you're drunk. And your dick is mediocre at best."

I scoffed. "Is that why you moan my name so loud when you're riding it? Because it's mediocre?"

I earned myself a full smile with that one. Drunk Me was on fire tonight.

"Whatever. I'm still not letting you up. My sister is here visiting, and she's asleep on the floor. I'm not about to have sex with you while she's in the room."

Pressing a hand to my chest, I tried to look affronted. "Imogen, I'm not a piece of meat for you to man-handle any time you like. I just came here to snuggle."

She snorted a laugh. "You just offered to show me your dick."

I glanced behind me, looking around the yard. "That wasn't me. You must have me confused with somebody else. I'm just here to snuggle the shit out of you, but if you're not into that, I guess I'll go..."

Silence hung between us and I shuddered against the cold. I'd left my jacket somewhere tonight. I couldn't remember where, but wherever it was I hoped it was having a good time.

Imogen sighed. "Fine. Come to the front door."

She didn't have to ask me twice. I bolted around the side of the townhouse to the front door like a little kid chasing an ice cream truck.

Imogen appeared at the door a moment later, her skin-tight tank top paired with the smallest, hottest sleep shorts I'd ever seen. The second she opened the door wide enough, I was inside, my body pressing against hers and my hands pawing her perfect ass.

"These are some amazing pajamas you've got here."

My mouth dipped to her throat, my lips moving across her skin with a desperation I'd never felt before. I wanted her, all the time, any way I could have her.

"Bant," she said, half chastising, half breathy.

"Mmm?" I murmured against her throat.

"We can't do this, you need to be quiet. I don't want to wake Stella or my sister."

A light snapped on over the stairs, Stella standing at the top with a smile on her face.

"Too late."

Imogen sighed louder and longer than I'd ever heard her. "There's nothing to see here."

Stella's grin widened. "Oh, I beg to differ. There is a whole lot to see here." She nodded at me. "Hey Bant."

"Stell."

I didn't remove my hands from Imogen's ass, mostly because it felt amazing in my palms, and we were already busted anyway. Besides, I'd caught Stella and Van in enough compromising positions last year that I owed them at least four awkward encounters before we were anywhere close to square.

Stella's grin was almost bursting off her face. "What an interesting little development this is, Imogen."

Imogen removed my hands from her ass, holding me by

the wrist and towing me up the stairs. "Please don't make a big deal about this, we're just sleeping together."

Stella pressed her lips together to fight her laugh as we passed her. "Whatever you say, love birds."

I winked at Stell over my shoulder as Imogen shut the door to her room.

It was dark inside but I could drunkenly make out an inflatable mattress on the floor, the sounds of light breathing coming from it.

"Do not wake my sister," Imogen hissed, pushing me down until I was sitting on the bed. Then she climbed in on her side. "And we're not having sex."

I toed off my shoes and tugged at the neck of my t-shirt, pulling it over my head. My jeans were off just as fast, leaving me in just my boxers as I slid in beside her.

"I meant it when I said I was just here to cuddle."

I pulled the blankets up over us and moved in until my long body was flush with hers. She was warm and soft, and I sighed as I wrapped my arms around her.

Hell yeah, this was everything I wanted.

"Imogen?" I whispered in the dark.

"Yeah?"

I pressed my lips against her hair, inhaling her vanilla shampoo. "Go out with me."

I could hear the smile in her voice when she whispered back. "Do you ever give up?"

"Not when it comes to you."

She was silent, and I tightened my arms around her, running the tip of my nose gently along the sensitive skin behind her ear.

"Come on, Im. Go out with me. Let me show you how much I like you."

She shook her head in the dark, only this time I could

handle the rejection. Because, while she was knocking me back again, we'd progressed from the eye rolling brushoffs she'd started at, which meant maybe she was coming around to the idea.

Or maybe that was wishful thinking on my part.

She twisted in my arms, snuggling closer against my chest until there wasn't an inch of space between us, her legs entwined with mine.

I fell asleep more blissed out than I'd been in a long time.

FOURTEEN

IMOGEN

I WOKE the next morning cold.

Rolling over, I searched for the human hot water bottle who had occupied my bed for half the night, only the space empty.

Had he bailed on me before I'd woken up when we hadn't even slept together?

When I stretched and sat up, the air mattress in the corner that Lola had slept in last night was empty too.

Throwing on a baggy sweatshirt, I padded down the stairs in search of her, the voices coming from the kitchen stopping me in the hall.

"So, you're coming to Pierson next year, huh?" came Bant's deep voice.

"Can't happen soon enough," Lola said. "With the way our parents are behaving, I'm desperate to get out of there."

"They're having a rough time?"

I gripped the edge of the doorway, staying out of sight and waiting for Lola's reply.

"More like a rough year, they've been at each other for a while. My sisters and I can't work out where they went wrong. They used to be so in love, then suddenly overnight it was like they weren't anymore. I have no idea what triggered it."

A stool scraped across the floor.

"Maybe life got in the way? Bills and jobs and schedules, all that stress?"

Lola sighed. "Maybe. I hope that's all it is and not, like... cheating or anything."

My eyebrows shot up. Lola and I had never discussed the possibility that one of our parents might have been unfaithful. Was that really what she thought was going on?

"It's a shame your sister and I are graduating at the end of the year. I could have taken you under my wing, shown you all the best places on campus, who to date and who to avoid on the basketball team."

Lola's laugh filled the kitchen. "Thanks, but I think I'd do better on my own."

Bant's answering chuckle floated through the door and Stella's whispered voice behind me made me jump.

"Your sister's bonding with the guy you're 'just hooking up with'. What a cute scene to wake up to for a commitment-phobe like you."

I whirled on her. "It's... whatever."

A smile spread across her face and she tilted her head to the side, studying me. "Ooooh, it is working on you. You're starting to like him!"

"No, I'm not. It's just sex."

"Great. So how was the sex last night?"

I levelled her with a look. "Obviously we didn't have sex with Lola in the same room."

Stella crossed her arms over her chest, delight radiating off her. "So, he came over here to snuggle and you let him in knowing full well that's all you'd be able to do? Tell me again that it's just sex, you little liar."

Ugh, as much as I loved her, her observations, no matter how correct they may be, were wholly unwelcome when I was doing my best to convince myself I felt nothing for Bant at all.

"Would you stop?"

"Just admit that it's more than sex and I'll think about it."

I threw my hands up, fighting a smile. "I'm not admitting to anything because there's nothing to admit to."

Her expression softened. "There's nothing wrong with liking him, Im. It's Bant, he's a catch. And your sister seems to like him too."

She gave me a pointed look, then moved past me into the kitchen, her cheery voice praising Bant and Lola for the pancakes they were cooking as the smell of chocolate chips filled the house.

Okay, so maybe Stella was right. There was the slight possibility I was starting to fall for Bant.

But there was no way in hell I was going to admit it out loud.

FIFTEEN

IMOGEN

BANT'S tall body curved over me from behind, his lips brushing my skin as he leaned down the murmur in my ear. "What's your favorite number?"

I bit my lip, relishing the feel of him against me. "Sixteen."

He nodded at the O'Reilly's bartender. "Sixteen vodka sodas."

My eyes widened.

"Really keen to get drunk tonight, Bant?" Lola asked, staring at him like she didn't know if he was a romantic Romeo or showboating ball player. Maybe a little of both.

He grinned. "They're for your sister, but I'm sure she'd be willing to share them with you if you ask really, really nicely. Maybe beg a little."

The guy behind the bar recruited another bartender and together they lined up two rows of eight lowball glasses, filling each with ice, then pouring out the alcohol.

"Sixteen drinks, boss, all yours," the bartender said and Bant handed over the cash.

He picked up two glasses, handing one each to Lola and I.

"You're insane, you know that?" I said with a disbelieving smile, glancing at the drinks lined up beside me on the bar.

He leaned in, his mouth brushing my cheek. "You're worth it."

A shiver skittered down my spine at the contact. Something had definitely shifted between us since he'd spent the night in my bed. He was softer with me, more affectionate. And I refused to admit how much I liked it.

Some guy called his name across the room and he gave them a nod, excusing himself to go to talk to them.

Lola grinned at me. "He's so into you, you know that, right?"

I took a sip of my drink. "He's into sleeping with me."

She gave me a look that said 'get a fucking clue'.

"No, Im, he's into you. What college ball player does something like this..." she motioned to the row of drinks beside us. "...for a girl whose pants he's already been in?"

I shrugged. "So, he's into me today. Doesn't mean he will be tomorrow. Like you said, he's a college ball player. He goes through women like water."

She sipped from her straw. "Or he's trying to woo you."

I choked on my drink, coughing. "Wow, you really are a hopeless romantic, Lol. Emphasis on the *hopeless*. Guys like Bant don't woo girls, they get what they want and bolt."

She shook her head, looking at me like I was a lost cause.

We fell into a comfortable silence, taking in the busy bar. I scanned to the room, eyes landing on Bant as he laughed with his friends. It was annoying how attractive he was. So many girls in the room were eyeing him like he was a piece of steak they wanted to devour for dinner and I hated it.

I shouldn't care. But despite my better judgment, I found I did.

A group of girls joined Bant and his friends and I turned back to my sister, determined to ignore the small inkling of jealousy rising inside me.

Bant wasn't mine. He could flirt with whoever he liked.

"So..." I said, working out the best way to bring up the situation between our parents. "I heard you with Bant in the kitchen this morning. Do you really think cheating might be the issue between Mom and Dad?"

She let out a heavy sigh. "I don't know, I can't figure it out. But why else would their marriage go from happy to volatile so fast?"

"Have either of them said anything to you about it?"

She shook her head. "They're too busy going at each other."

I grimaced, my stomach tightening. Our parents and the connection they shared had been so solid growing up, the perfect foundation to our family unit. The idea that foundation might be crumbling beneath us filled me with a sense of dread.

My parents had always been my example of what I wanted out of a future partner and a long-lasting relationship. After my string of failed relationships, their union gave me hope. But if their love was a lie, what chance was there for the rest of us? And what would our family become if my parents weren't together? Separate holidays, separate birthdays, totally separate lives?

I hated the idea.

I was about to tell Lola as much when someone stumbled into her and she almost emptied her drink down my front, both of us gripping her glass to steady it.

"Oh shit, I'm so sorry," the guy said, swivelling in our direction.

He was tall and lean, with bright green eyes and thick dark brown hair. Undeniably hot, yet also undeniably not my type. Because apparently my type was now a six-foot-four blond basketball player with a monster dick, a magic tongue, and a menagerie of eager girls following him wherever he went. Clearly, I was a sucker for heartbreak.

Lola smiled back at the guy and I knew that look. She was half-smitten just at the sight of him.

Jesus, she really is a hopeless romantic.

"I'm Aaron." He offered her his hand, giving her a once-over that most definitely said he was just as interested in my little sister. "But everyone calls me Cookie."

Lola returned the handshake. "Cute."

He smiled. "Me or the nickname?"

Wow, these two weren't messing around. I suddenly felt like one hell of a third wheel. I leaned against the bar, my chin propped up in my hand, content to watch the romance reality TV show playing out in front of me.

"Maybe both?" Lola took a sip of her drink, a coquettish smile on her face. "Why does everyone call you Cookie?"

Aaron shifted closer. "I'd like to say there's an amazing story behind it, like I'm an aspiring pastry chef and cookies are my specialty. Then I could offer to make them for you, invite you round to my place. It'd be a cute first date for us."

Lola's face split into a broad smile.

Oh, for the love of god. Was I going to have to worry about her alone at Pierson next year after I graduated if she fell for lines like that so easily?

"But I'm not that interesting," Aaron said, running a hand through his hair, his eyes never leaving Lola. "My last name is Cooke."

I was about to ruin the moment with a remark about what a letdown the truth really was, when Bant appeared behind me, the warmth of him melting into my back. The move was far too coupley and possessive for our current situation, but I relished the feel of him and a small part of me was happy he was no longer surrounded by women who weren't me.

He leaned over my shoulder, his other hand gripping my hip possessively, and offered Aaron a bro slap.

"Cookie, man. How's the season?"

Lola glanced between Bant and Aaron. "The season?"

Aaron shoved his hands in the pockets of his jeans, giving a shrug. "Swim team."

My sister practically swooned at discovering he was an athlete.

Way to play it cool, Lol.

"Don't let him play it down, he's the captain. Cookie is part fish in the pool."

He leaned in close to Lola like he was sharing a secret. "I prefer part shark."

The guy was smooth, I'd give him that. But my sister was still in high school and Aaron was no freshman. She was only in this bar because of one very convincing fake ID.

"Whatever you say, bro." Bant clapped Aaron on the shoulder, turning to the bar and picking up two of the vodka sodas, handing one to him.

Cookie gratefully accepted, turning his attention to Lola, the two of them falling into easy conversation.

I nudged Bant in the ribs. "I thought those were for me.

Now you're handing them out to smooth swim bros trying to win over my sister?"

His eyes lit with humor. "Swim bros? And they're all yours, but you should have picked a smaller number. There's no way you're getting through them all at the rate you're going. You've been nursing that same one for half an hour."

"I didn't realise we were in a hurry tonight."

He shifted closer, invading my space with his body, his hands on either side of me pinning me to the bar. "I'm in a hurry to get you naked in the supply closet out back, I know that much."

"That might just be the most romantic thing any guy has ever said to me." I rolled my eyes, downing my drink and picking up another.

"The alley by the dumpster then?" he tried, chuckling when I shoved him in the shoulder.

My expression twisted with mock outrage. "You're disgusting and desperate, and I can't stand you."

He ducked his head, lips ghosting across my temple in the softest kiss. "That's a lie. You love it when I give you a hard time. You get off on it, in fact. So much so you're actually starting to like me back."

I bit the inside of my cheek, enjoying the way his mouth moved from my temple along the sensitive skin behind my ear, and down my throat. My body reacted to him all on its own, firing up inside when his hands slid over my waist and down to cup my ass.

That supply closet was looking pretty good right now. Maybe even the alleyway would do. But I was a lady, I wasn't actually going to bone down with Bant in a dirty back alley or in among the mops.

"It's cute that you think I'm the kind of girl who'd get it on anywhere."

He shrugged. "I think you're the kind of girl who knows what she wants at all times and isn't afraid to take it."

I wished that were true. The reality was far more depressing; I was afraid. I'd put my trust in the wrong guys too many times and now I was too scared to trust even my own judgment or get in any deeper than casual hook-ups.

But did I want to be different with Bant?

It was too soon to tell. Or maybe I was just doing what I always did.

Keeping my heart so protected I wasn't sure it was still there.

SIXTEEN

BANT

GROUP CHAT: *Big Ballers w Bigger Balls* 2.0 (*The Bigger the Better*)

HERNANDEZ: Who's up for pizza and beer at the basketball house tonight?

DAVIS: In

BANT: In

LI: Definitely in

HOOKER: Hard in

MONTY: I've got a big writing project due, but I'll pop downstairs for a slice at some point.

STELLA: In

JERICHO: In

HERNANDEZ: What about Imogen?

STELLA: She says she's a no. Had a bad day, wants to throw on some sweats and hang out at home.

DAVIS: Is it that time of the month?

LI: For fuck's sake Davis, you can't ask girls that

DAVIS: It's my right to know so I can avoid them at all costs.

JERICHO: Not asking that question is an unwritten rule if you want to keep your nutsack attached to your body.

HOOKER: It's no surprise he's single…

DAVIS: With my stunning good looks, it's very surprising actually.

HERNANDEZ: Yo Bant, can you grab the pizzas on your way home?

BANT: Change of plans, can't make it

DAVIS: Dude…

I PULLED up outside Stella and Imogen's townhouse, reaching for the pizza box on the seat beside me.

A night of pizza and beer with the guys had sounded appealing, right up until Stella had said Imogen had a bad day and planned to sit on the couch alone. Imogen was always up for spending time with her friends and never missed a chance to hang shit on my teammates at the basketball house, which meant something was up if she was choosing this instead.

There was a chance she'd take one look at me on her doorstep holding a pizza and shut the door in my face, but it was a risk I was willing to take. There was no way I was going to sit at home watching my teammates get wasted, wondering if she was okay.

Climbing the couple of steps to her front door, I rang the bell and waited. Footsteps shuffled inside and then the door opened, revealing Imogen in baggy sweats, a baggier hoodie and her hair piled on top of her head in a ponytail.

She looked hot as fuck, even swimming in her sweats, and I wanted to toss the pizza in the garden like a damn frisbee and make her come right here on the entryway floor.

But tonight wasn't about me.

She was down and I was here to lift her up. Not get her into bed.

"Bant..." Her eyes roamed me, snagging on the pizza in my hands. "What are you doing here?"

"Stell said you had a bad day. I didn't want you to be alone."

She stared back at me, a slight pinch in her brow. Then it smoothed out just as fast and she stepped aside, opening the door wide to let me in.

I tried to tamp down the swell of victory in my chest that she hadn't immediately told me to get lost. Maybe my charm was working on her. Maybe she was finally going to let me into more than just her bed.

I strode into the living room, Imogen following behind.

"How long you can stay will be determined by what toppings you ordered on that pizza." She gave me a wry smile, motioning to the box, and I flipped it open with nothing but confidence.

"Pepperoni, red peppers and pineapple."

She stared back at me in disbelief. "How did you...?"

I grinned. "I asked Monty what your favorite pizza toppings were. Although, I have to say, pineapple on pizza, Im? You're on friendship probation with that food choice."

She snagged a slice from the box and sat on the couch with her feet tucked under her.

"Judge me, I dare you," she said around a mouthful,

letting out a small moan as she chewed. "Oh my god, this is exactly what I needed."

I flopped down on the other end of the couch. "Glad I could provide it."

She glanced at me out of the corner of her eye. "I thought for sure you were going to make some smart remark about providing me with your dick to fuck my bad day away."

I snorted. "I'm not some horndog that's only out to get my dick wet every minute of the day."

She gave me a pointed look.

"Come on," I said with a laugh, only slightly affronted. "I do have dreams beyond getting laid, you know."

She took another bite. "Basketball?"

I sprawled on the couch, getting comfortable. "Nah. Basketball I do for fun."

Surprise lit her face. "Really? I thought you, Van and West were all about the NBA."

"Van and West are. It's all they've wanted for as long as I've known them, so I'm stoked they've made it all the way. But going pro has never been my goal."

"You've set the goal of sleeping your way around campus, instead?"

Her expression was full of humor, but I couldn't help but wonder if she really believed that bedding a bunch of girls was all I was interested in. Or how much of her obsession with my extracurricular activities was actually about me. I knew her ex had cheated on her and Stella had mentioned that it wasn't the first time something like that had happened to her. Being cheated on more than once had to mean she was harboring some serious trust issues.

I had my own trust issues going on too. The situation with Delaney had messed me up more than I cared to admit. It had changed my mind entirely about relationships in college and altered the way I interacted with women.

"You really don't think much of me, do you?" I tried, reaching for a slice of pizza and sitting back on the couch.

She shrugged, giving me a small smile. "The pizza has helped you grow in my estimation."

I raised a brow in response, but on the inside I was celebrating that she'd actually admitted I was growing on her.

"In all seriousness, I'm not here to try to get in your pants. You had a bad day, I didn't want you to be alone. That's the only reason I'm here."

She studied me, searching my face for the lie, her voice quiet when she spoke.

"Well... thank you."

I nodded, reaching for the remote on the cushion between us.

"So, what are we binge-watching?"

SEVENTEEN

IMOGEN

"THIS ISN'T how I imagined spending my Thursday night," Bant said from where he was sprawled on my couch.

His head was resting on the back and his long legs were stretched out in front of him on the coffee table, crossed at the ankles like he didn't have a care in the world. He picked up a chocolate from the tray between us, popping it in his mouth and chewing happily.

I tried not to laugh at how ridiculous he looked with my green seaweed face mask spread all over his skin.

Stella had been right. That night he'd turned up outside my window had changed everything for me. It was as though falling asleep with his arms wrapped around me had unlocked something inside me and I was finding it more difficult every minute I spent with him to keep my feelings —and my hands — to myself.

I worked to ignore the way my body itched to be closer

to him. I wanted to shuffle down the couch and straddle his lap. Instead, I forced myself to stay put.

"Face masks, pizza and sitting on the couch in my sweats? This night is as close to my definition of perfect as it can get."

His gaze landed on mine. "Any night with you is as close to perfect as it gets for me."

My cheeks heated and silence hung between us, along with a charged kind of tension, and I turned away, fumbling for the closest chocolate in the tray and shoving it in my mouth before I could say something I'd regret.

Bant watched me, the hint of a smile tugging at his mouth, before he turned back to the Schitt's Creek re-run playing on the TV. We watched in comfortable silence, Bant's laughter filling the room, his enormous body shaking the couch.

"Time to rinse."

I dragged him to the bathroom, positioning him so that we were standing side-by-side at the mirror.

Bant studied me as I scrubbed the green from my skin, my face almost wiped clean. I handed him a fresh cloth and he stared down at it like I'd given him a Rubik's cube and asked him to solve it in three seconds flat.

"What am I supposed to do with that?"

"Wipe yourself off, you weirdo."

He pulled a face. "With that scratchy thing? It'll hurt."

I turned to face him, propping my hip against the counter. "You're being such a man-baby. Do you want to stay green and have the opposing team at your game tomorrow night call you Shrek when you take the court?"

He looked affronted, reaching for the bottom of his hoodie and yanking it up to reveal his stacked abs. "Does this look like Shrek to you?"

I glanced at the perfect divots in his stomach, swallowing hard. So what if I wanted to glide my tongue over every peak and valley of his hard torso? It didn't mean anything.

I turned away, trying to pretend the sight didn't affect me at all.

Definitely not Shrek.

Bant smirked. "Didn't think so."

I rolled my eyes. "Well, if you don't take the mask off, that's what they're going to call you."

"You do it."

I knew it was a ploy for us to get closer, to establish some kind of physical connection, and I wanted to protest. To tell him he was being a man baby again and remind him he was more than capable of wiping his own face.

But I stopped myself.

Was it really worth fighting him on? And what would denying him prove?

He'd turned up here tonight because he heard I was down, then spent the night doing boring, girly stuff with me to build me back up. So far, not only had he not complained, it seemed like he might just be enjoying himself. And if I were being honest with myself, I was too.

When we weren't sniping at each other and I wasn't spending every minute trying to push him away, I found I actually liked spending time with him. And not just between the sheets.

Luke Bantempelli may be a raging playboy at Pierson, but underneath all the ego was a guy who was sweet and sensitive and attentive.

So maybe, just this once, I could concede something between us.

That didn't stop me from sighing dramatically to cover

how I really felt. Admitting to myself that maybe I was starting to like Bant was one thing. There was no reason to let him know it.

Taking the cloth, I ran it under warm water, squeezing it out and reaching up to wipe at his cheek.

"You're so tall," I complained, turning back to the faucet to rinse out the cloth a second time.

When I turned back around, he'd moved closer, his hands landing gently on my hips, sending a jolt through me. He stared down at me and I suddenly found it hard to breathe.

"I can fix that."

He backed me towards the counter, lifting me up so I was sitting on it. Then he nudged my knees apart with his hips, moving to stand between my legs. He leaned down so his hands were splayed on the counter either side of my waist, his face inches from mine.

"Better?"

I swallowed against the sudden tightness in my throat, nodding.

Ignoring the bout of desire sweeping through me, I gently wiped the warm cloth over his skin, the green mask coming off in streaks to reveal his perfect face. He looked like an athletic Austin Butler. Only hotter, if that were even possible.

He watched me, blue eyes trained on mine the entire time, his face so close I could feel his warm breath on my skin.

"Your eyes are incredible," he said, his low voice making my core clench.

I paused, fighting the urge to pull away or shut him down with some snarky comeback.

"Yours aren't bad either."

He chuckled. "How much did it pain you to say something nice to me?"

I couldn't help my smile, wiping at his face again. "More than you know."

We fell silent, his eyes studying me as I worked, making me want to squirm.

"I like you," he said eventually.

"You've mentioned that once or twice."

"Well, it's still true."

"I'm sure you like a lot of girls."

His gaze softened. "There's no one like you, Imogen."

My hand stilled at his cheek, and I studied him.

I hated what his words were doing to me. I didn't want to fall for him, I wanted to be immune to him. But he was nothing like I'd thought he was. The overconfident playboy was definitely a part of him, but it wasn't all of him. He had so much more to offer and that was just from the glimpses of the real him he'd shown me so far.

What would it be like to date him? Would he be the kind of guy who opened doors and cooked me dinner and showed up after class just to walk me across campus? Something told me that's exactly who he'd be. But the protective part of me stopped me from letting myself truly open up. I'd been burned so many times, I wasn't sure I even knew how to be truly open with someone anymore.

He turned his head, his lips brushing the inside of my wrist that was still hovering near his face. The sweetness of it startled me into stillness.

"I..."

Didn't know what to say. There was no way I could get involved with a guy like Bant, my heart couldn't handle it. He had a new girl following him around or fawning over him every day. I didn't want to be another one in a long line. Or worse, the jealous girlfriend who couldn't trust him.

Only... what would it be like to have those strong arms wrapped around me and those lips murmuring sweet words across my skin every night? What would it be like to walk through campus with his arm slung around my shoulders, everyone knowing we were together? I'd seen what Monty and Stella had with West and Van and I wanted that too. I just didn't know how to get it without opening myself up to the kind of heartbreak I was so used to.

I turned away, dropping the cloth in the sink and forcing a smile on my face. "You're all clean."

I slid from the counter, forcing him back a step. I strode for the door like it wasn't taking every ounce of willpower I had to walk away from him.

It didn't matter how much I liked the idea of being with Bant. Dating him was a terrible idea. One that had the potential to ruin me.

I made it three steps before he snagged my wrist, gently tugging me back to him. His arms wrapped around my waist and my hands landed on his strong chest, closing over the soft material of his sweatshirt.

He dropped his head, planting the softest kiss against my throat. "Go out with me, Im."

He was more serious than I'd ever heard him. And I so desperately wanted to say yes this time.

"Forget all the reasons you've convinced yourself you shouldn't, take a chance and trust me. Say yes."

I bit my lip, staring back at him. Those blue eyes were pleading, his expression filled with a softness I've never seen from him before. He was being vulnerable with me and laying his cards out on the table. I wanted to meet him halfway but I was so scared that taking that leap with him—

with anyone—would come back to hurt me, just as it had so many times in the past.

But maybe Bant wasn't those guys, no matter how much I'd tried to convince myself he was exactly like them. If I wanted to be happy, at some point I was going to have to put my heart on the line again. Either Bant was worth it or he wasn't. It was time to decide or let him go.

Swallowing down my fear, I tugged on his sweatshirt, slowly pulling his mouth down to mine, giving him an answer just before our lips touched.

"Fine, I'll go out with you."

His face lit with a ruinous grin.

Then he kissed me like he couldn't survive without it.

EIGHTEEN

BANT

"SHIT."

I swore at my phone, reading the text message from Renee as I left the locker room post-practice.

Hooker stopped just inside the door to the parking lot at the end of the hall. "Everything okay, dude?"

Renee had texted me an SOS, which meant something was going down at the shelter. Did that mean her ex had found them?

"I don't know, man, but I've gotta go. Can you get a ride with Davis?"

I didn't wait for his reply, just pushed through the doors and was across the parking lot to my car in an instant.

Renee and Kelsie deserved peace. Renee had gone through hell to get them out of that house and away from her abusive ex. I prayed to every god in every religion possible he hadn't hunted them down. There was no way in hell I was going to let him hurt them again.

Ten minutes later, I pulled up in the parking lot out the back of the shelter, not bothering to check whether I was in the space or not. I shut the car off and bolted for the back door, hauling it open. Raven was in the kitchen with two of the other kitchenhands.

"What's happening, Raven?"

Her head popped up in relief. "Oh, Luke. Kelsie will be so happy to see you. I think it's all going down out front."

I bolted out of the kitchen and into the dining hall, some of the shelter residents watching over a group of kids who were playing in the corner, Kelsie among them. Her face lit up when she spotted me.

"Luke!"

I crouched down before she reached me, my arms wide. She ran into them, clinging to my shoulder.

"He found us. My daddy, he found us."

I patted her back, making soothing noises. "Don't you worry about that, Kels. The grown-ups will take care of it, okay?"

She pulled back, her little face filled with anxiety. "Is he going to hurt me and my mommy again?"

I shook my head. "No way, kid."

And I meant it. There was no way that dirtbag was coming anywhere near Kelsie or Renee.

"I'm going to go find your mom, okay? You stay with the other kids."

She nodded, reluctantly letting me go, and I pushed to my feet, hustling down the halls of the shelter to the front lobby.

I heard the commotion before I saw it, a man shouting about being given what was his. I rounded the corner to find Hadiza and Marie, two of the shelter directors attempting to block the guy's path. How he'd managed to get through the first two sets of locked security doors, I had no idea, but he wouldn't be making it any further.

"What's going on?" I asked, squaring my shoulders and stretching to my full height.

He was tall and broad, with thinning brown hair and a sneer plastered on his face. I had a few inches on him, and I'd use any tactic I could to intimidate the bastard and get him to back off.

"Oh, and who's this guy? Some young hotshot my bitch wife is boning behind my back?"

My jaw tightened at the slight against Renee. This guy was a serious piece of work, up there with the best of them. Not only did he knock his wife and kid around, but that was the way he spoke about them?

"Get the fuck out of here, buddy." I pointed to the doors in case the guy was a moron too and didn't understand basic instructions.

He scowled at me. "I'm not your fucking buddy. And I'll leave as soon as I get my wife and kid."

"That's not going to happen," I said, taking a step towards him.

He didn't back down, meeting me toe to toe.

"Oh yeah? And who the hell's going to stop me? You, pretty boy?"

I huffed a humorless laugh. "You're damn right I am. You have no right to storm in here making demands. Whoever you're looking for, they're not here. You've been given shit information. So, take your threats and your shitty haircut and get the fuck out before the cops arrive."

I didn't have to ask to know Marie or Hadiza would have called them the second this guy set foot inside the shelter.

"I don't know who you think you are, kid. But I'll leave

when I've got what I came for. Now get the fuck out of my face before I mess yours up."

This guy was a textbook bully, throwing his weight around and issuing threats in an effort to intimidate me. But I'd wised up to those tactics by the time I was six, thanks to the shitty dad life had handed me. One just like this guy.

"You can take all the swings at me you want. It won't change the fact that the people you're looking for aren't here."

He moved closer, eyes narrowed and jaw tight, getting in my face. "I didn't really mean it before, but now I wonder if maybe I was right. Are you sleeping with her? Did she open her legs for you like she always does?"

I didn't hesitate, swinging my fist and connecting with his face.

His cheekbone gave a satisfying crack, his head snapping to the side. Pain seared through my knuckles but I didn't have it in me to care. The piece of shit deserved to feel what it was like to be on the receiving end of a hit for a change.

Before I could even reconcile what I'd done, he clocked me hard in the face, my eye socket bursting with pain. I stumbled, but righted myself fast, lunging for him and swinging a fist at his mid-section. He let out a grunt, but returned the favor, dishing out a swift punch to my ribs.

Fuck me, that one is going to bruise.

I gripped him in a headlock, determined to make minced meat out of his face. He fought back with a surprising amount of strength and we hit the floor, both of us scrambling to get the upper hand. Only I had daily basketball workouts and at least twenty years of youth on my side.

I gripped the front of his shirt with one hand, swinging

at his face with the other. He took the blow, then came right back for more, eyes burning with anger.

No wonder Renee and Kelsie were terrified of this guy. He was a brute with a serious case of rage.

He clawed at my arm, trying to shove me off, his fist connecting with my lip. Blood exploded from my split skin, dripping onto the guy's shirt, but I didn't release my grip. Instead, I hit him again, this time connecting with his jaw.

The door to the shelter buzzed open, a rush of feet behind me. I pulled back to swing at him, but strong hands gripped my arm, holding me back.

"That's enough, son. Let him go," a police officer ordered.

I obeyed, raising my hands and pushing to my feet, wincing at the pain in my side and face. Two officers rushed forward to haul Renee's ex to his feet, blood running from his nose.

It didn't matter what kind of trouble I was in with the cops or how pissed Coach was going to be if I couldn't take the court this weekend.

Defending Renee and Kelsie was worth it.

NINETEEN

IMOGEN

HE WAS TWENTY MINUTES LATE.

I glanced around Ruby's diner, trying not to appear as uncomfortable as I felt sitting on my own in a packed restaurant, waiting for what was clearly meant to be a date.

When I'd finally agreed to go out with Bant, he'd let me choose the place and I'd picked Ruby's because, even if the date was bad, at least I'd get a decent burger out of it.

Only... I knew the date wasn't going to be bad.

The sex between us was more phenomenal than I'd ever admit to his face, and Bant and I had never had a problem with conversation before, even if in the past it had been fuelled by a complete disdain for each other. Things had changed between us after he turned up on my doorstep drunk and as difficult as it was for me to admit it, I liked this new version of us.

I liked him. Which was why I'd finally agreed to go to dinner with him.

And now... *he wasn't here.*

I shoved aside that ugly little voice inside me that said I never should have trusted him in the first place and checked my phone for the fifth time, trying not to look like I'd been stood up.

Nothing.

"Not often I see you sitting all alone..." came a voice from beside me, and I glanced up, hiding my phone beneath the table.

Of course Jackson was here right now, because that's just what I needed.

"I'm waiting for someone," I said, trying to sound as casual as I could muster with shame coursing through me.

"It looks like they might have stood you up." A slow smile spread across his face. "I'd never stand you up."

I reached for my soda, taking a sip and forcing myself to smile back at him.

"I'm sure." I waved my phone at him. "But they just sent me a text to say they're on their way."

A blatant lie. My phone was quieter than the library during finals.

Someone called Jackson's name from across the diner and he turned his head to nod, before glancing back at me. "My offer of a date is still on the table, and I'll actually show up."

He knocked his knuckle against the tabletop then sauntered back to his friends.

My jaw clenched.

Damn it, Bant.

Where the hell are you?

My better judgment had told me to stay away from him, to stay away from all guys because none of them could be trusted. College boys told you what you wanted to hear to get you into bed with them—or in this case, agree to a date with him— and then ghosted you without so much as an 'I'm sorry' Snap. All the warning signs had been there, and I'd brushed them aside and opened myself up to heartbreak and humiliation again. Surely that made me the biggest fool on campus.

How had I let myself get sucked in by a hot mouth, a sweet smile, and tight set of abs?

I was better than this. I *knew* better than this.

My phone lit up on the table and I snatched it up, unlocking it.

BANT: *Can't make it tonight. I'm sorry.*

What the actual fuck?

He was bailing on me thirty minutes after he was supposed to be here?

He'd been trying for months to get me to go out with him. I finally said yes and now I was sitting here alone at the damn diner without so much as an explanation.

The fucking audacity.

Embarrassment burned through me as I collected my phone and bag, throwing some money on the table to pay for the soda and a tip.

I never should have agreed to this. I never should have let my guard down.

Rushing from the diner, I pushed through the door into the chilled night air.

He'd probably bailed on me to hook up with some jersey chaser. I bet the two of them were at the basketball house right now, going at it on every surface, since most of his teammates were at a party over on jock row with Stella and Monty.

There was no way in hell I was letting him off that easy, I was going to go over there and give him a piece of my mind. I didn't give a damn if it meant I might be interrupting his precious time with some basketball bunny. Bant was going to learn exactly what I thought about him and the bullshit romance routine I'd make him regret ever pulling on me.

I jumped in my car, anger fuelling me the entire way to the basketball house. By the time I arrived I was a woman on a mission, determined to tear him to shreds with all the ways he'd wronged me, and maybe women everywhere.

I pounded on the door, my heart hammering in my chest as I stared out at the street. The neighbors were about to get a show.

Footsteps sounded on the other side and the door opened. I opened my mouth, ready to rip into him.

And froze at the sight of him.

His lip was cut, his eye swollen and purple and his hand was clutched to his right side. He shifted on his feet as I stared at him, wincing with pain at the movement, and all the anger rushed out of me at once.

"I know you're mad at me, but I can't right now, Im..."

He turned from the door, leaving it wide open, and limped back down the hall.

I shut the door behind me and hurried after him, finding him in the kitchen. "What happened to you?"

He moved gingerly to the freezer for an ice pack, hissing against the pain as he reached for it. I came around beside him, pulling it out for him and ushering him towards a seat at the counter. He didn't argue, sitting with a hiss.

"Got into a fight."

I wrapped the ice pack in the towel by the sink and moved in front of him, holding it to his eye. He pulled back, taking my hand in his and gently pressing it against his torso instead. He tipped his head back and groaned at the ceiling with what I think was a mix of annoyance and pain.

"It's a really long story."

I bit the inside of my cheek. I couldn't imagine Bant getting in a fight for the sake of it. He was the guy who liked to have a good time, the one who was all about fun, not fist fights. If he'd come to blows with someone, it had to be for a reason.

"I've got the time, if you want to tell me."

His gaze landed on me, clearly debating whether or not to trust me with the truth.

He sighed. "I volunteer at the women's shelter in town. There's a mom and her kid who I'm close with, and her abusive husband tracked them there. He showed up demanding to see them. Wouldn't take no for an answer and insulted her, so I hit him."

I stared back at him.

I didn't know which piece of information to process first. The fact Bant volunteered at the women's shelter or that he'd put his own safety on the line to defend a mother and her child from their abuser.

He watched me, trying to gauge my reaction.

Slowly, I reached out and cupped a hand to his face— the side that wasn't swollen—and he leaned into the touch, blowing out an exhausted breath. He looked bone tired, like he needed to sleep for a week.

"I can't believe you did that..."

He gave me a weary smile. "Yeah, well... I know what it's like to grow up running from an abusive dad."

My heart stalled in my chest. "You do?"

He nodded.

"My mom finally got us out when I was eight. We lived in a shelter just like the one in town for a while, until my mom could get on her feet. I went down to the shelter here my first week at Pierson to volunteer. The people who work at those places change lives, they deserve all the help they can get."

I stared back at him, questioning everything I'd ever thought I'd known about him.

Womanising jocks only out for a good time didn't volunteer at women's shelters. They didn't open up about their painful pasts or fight abusers to protect an innocent mother and child. I didn't know this side of Bant at all. But I desperately wanted to.

"I had no idea..." I said quietly.

"Most people don't. It's not exactly something I broadcast, for my mom's sake as much as mine."

There was no missing the admiration he had for his mom when he spoke about her.

"She sounds like an incredible woman."

He gave me another small smile. "She is. Same as you."

A blush coloured my cheeks and I turned away from him to tidy up the counter. I never knew what to do with the sweet things he said. He delivered them so easily, as though for him, opening up took no effort at all. But they were even harder to accept when he was comparing me with his mom, a woman who had escaped a horrible relationship with her small child in tow to save them from a life of violence.

We were not the same. She was strong. I was just all kinds of messed up.

"How often do you go to the shelter?"

"As much as I can, usually a couple of times a week. Davis comes with me when he can."

"Can I come with you some time?"

His eyes connected with mine, an emotion I couldn't read swirling there. "Yeah... of course."

We stared at each other, a million different emotions passing between us. In this moment it was clear how little we really knew about each other. We'd spent so much time bickering, playing little power games to get under each other's skin, that we'd never really taken the time to get to know the real person behind the front we both put up to face the world.

"Come on, Rocky. Let's get you cleaned up. Those ribs need a warm bath."

He pulled a face. "Is this a ploy to get me naked? Because while I'm pretty useless right now, if you're willing to hook up with me, I'll make it work. Maybe you can ride me."

I huffed a laugh. "Still got your priorities straight I see, even when you're injured."

He pushed to his feet, throwing an arm around my shoulders, and I hugged his waist to help him hobble from the kitchen. "It was my face and ribs that took a beating, not my sex drive."

"Or your ego."

It took a good five minutes to climb the stairs, Bant wincing the whole way. We made it to the bathroom, and I perched him on the closed toilet while I ran him a hot bath, stealing some of Monty's scented bubble bath.

"This is a really elaborate ploy to get me naked," Bant said, with the ghost of his usual smirk.

He reached for my hand, his thumb brushing over my knuckles with a softness he'd never shown before.

"All you have to do is ask, Im. I want you anytime, anywhere."

I stared down at him, brushing a hand through his hair.

His eyes closed, some of the built-up tension visibly melting from him.

I'd stormed over here tonight, determined to tear him to shreds for standing me up. Instead, he'd shown me a piece of the real him. Things had already been moving fast between us lately and tonight felt like we were being plunged into warp speed.

It scared me.

But I was also melting at the way he was looking at me. And the way he leaned into my touch like he needed me.

I gave him a small smile, turning to check the temperature of the bath and shutting off the faucet. Hearing him talk about the shelter and defending the residents there had shifted something in me, and I didn't know how I was supposed to feel anymore. My emotions were almost always in check, usually hidden behind snarky comebacks or the hard walls I'd built around my heart a long time ago. I learned to harden myself against the actions of others so they couldn't hurt me. But only someone truly heartless would be immune to what Bant had done tonight. He was one of the good ones, and he was looking at me like he thought I was worthy of him.

I cleared my throat. "Bath's ready. Do you need help getting undressed?"

He glanced at the bath and then back at me. "You're going to make me get in there by myself?"

I frowned. "Bant, we're not both going to fit. You're huge."

He outright smirked this time and relief flooded me at the spark returning to his eyes.

"In height, not just in the pants, playboy. There isn't room for both of us."

He stood slowly and I helped him pull his shirt over his head.

"We'll fit. You get in first."

I paused, the pleading in his eyes my undoing. I sighed, tugging my shirt over my head. His gaze was hot against my skin as he watched me undress down to my black lace bralette and underwear.

"Do you mind?" I motioned for him to turn around.

He obeyed and I stripped and slid into the bubbles. He dropped his shorts, the beast between his legs right at face level again.

"I swear you're determined to take my eye out with that thing," I muttered.

He climbed in gingerly, cursing and huffing through the pain.

"There are so many other things... I'd rather do to you with it... than poke you in the eye... trust me on that."

I couldn't help my chuckle. He sank down in the water with his back to me, reaching behind him to spread my knees wide before he settled against me, his back to my chest and his head against my shoulder. He took my wrists, wrapping my arms around him until my hands were settled on his pecs.

He closed his eyes, with a satisfied sigh. "I feel better already."

"I'm glad one of us is comfortable."

"Oh please, don't even pretend like this isn't turning you on. All this slick skin and our warm bodies pressed together. I could die happy right now."

I reached for a shower sponge near my shoulder, dipping it in the water and slowly rubbing it over his body. "As long as you're comfortable. You might have cracked ribs."

He murmured blissfully in response to my touch. "Just bruised. I've cracked ribs before and it hurts a hell of a lot more than this."

"Basketball injury?"

He nodded, water sloshing at my neck. "Been playing since I was six. My poor mom has nursed me through just about every injury possible." He gave my knee a squeeze. "But this treatment is a hell of a lot better."

I smiled to myself.

"So, why isn't the NBA the goal for you?"

West and Van had been driven by a seemingly single-minded focus to make it to the pros. I knew Bant was good enough. I'd heard Monty and West talk about it. I'd been wondering about it since the night on the couch when he'd told me he wasn't interested in playing pro ball.

"I don't have the passion for it. I play basketball because I love it, going pro would steal the joy out of playing for me."

He was right. There was no point pursuing something you didn't love.

I trailed the sponge across his skin, dipping lower with each circle. "So, what's your plan then? Play college ball, then what?"

He swallowed hard, distracted by the movements of my hand. "Someone is chatty tonight..."

I laughed.

"... handsy too."

I lifted both my hands from the water. "I can stop if it's annoying you."

"Stop and you might get to see a grown man cry."

Smiling to myself, I dipped the sponge back in the water, sliding it over his torso, careful to avoid his right side.

His eyes closed and he let out a quiet groan when my

hand dipped low enough that the sponge brushed against the top of his hard length. "You're killing me worse than my injuries."

"Just trying to make you feel better." I trailed my free hand down the center of his chest and over the hard ridges of his abs, stretching to reach between his legs.

He groaned, tipping his head back against my shoulder. "Whatever kind of therapy this is, I'm going to need you to provide it every day for the next week."

I smiled to myself, relishing the effect I was having on him. "You haven't answered my question..."

"You asked a question? All I can think about is your hand near my dick and how much I want it."

Sweeping my fingers back over his abs and up the center of his chest, he groaned again, this time in frustration.

"What do you want to do after college?"

I slowly trailed my hand back down his torso and he swallowed.

"Player manager," he croaked, but I barely heard it.

"Sorry... what was that?"

Discarding the sponge in water, I brushed my fingers along the underside of his cock, making it spring upwards in the water.

"Player... manager," he ground out, his eyes closing when my fingers brushed over him again.

"So, you want to represent sports players? Negotiate billion-dollar contracts for them?"

He nodded, eyes still closed, his teeth sinking into his bottom lip.

"For any players? Or just NBA players like West and Van?"

I sat forward a little, as much as I could manage with his

back pressed against my chest, and wrapped my hand around his shaft.

"Fuck, Imogen, I really don't want to talk about my friends right now."

I bit my lip, fighting another smile and loving the way he was reacting to me.

"What do you want to talk about then?"

"Not a thing. I want to..."

He went to turn over in the water to face me, remembering his injured ribs and letting out a grunt of pain.

"Maybe we should get out?" I offered.

He nodded, struggling upright so I could slide out from behind him. I secured a towel around my body, before helping him from the tub.

He smirked at me while I rubbed him down with a towel and helped him hobble into his bedroom.

I pointed to the mattress. "You. On the bed."

"Yes, ma'am. You should be this bossy in the bedroom all the time."

With a whole lot more groaning, he managed to get himself on the bed. He stared up at the ceiling, and I tried not to drool at the sight of him totally naked and sprawled there.

He's injured, Imogen. Calm down.

He lifted his head, eyes filled with heat. "Come over here."

When I walked to the side of the bed, he gripped the bottom of the towel, tugging on it and letting it drop to the floor. His eyes roamed my body, his gaze sparking at the sight.

I climbed on the bed, careful as I straddled him, his hard cock pressing between my legs. His palm smoothed over my breast, making my nipple peak. He toyed with the hard bud, running his thumb over it in circles, then he gripped my waist and nudged me forward. I leaned closer and he took my nipple in his mouth, sucking and biting at it, making my body sing with pleasure. He palmed my other breast, before swapping sides, his mouth doing amazing things.

"You have the most incredible tits."

He rubbed his thumbs over both of them, and heat pooled at my core. My hips started to move against him and he held my waist, rocking me, both of us moaning in unison at the delicious friction.

I leaned down to kiss him, his mouth opening for me, our tongues sweeping together in slow, easy strokes that had my core tightening once more.

Hard, fast, hot sex with Bant was amazing. But this was something else entirely.

His touch was unhurried, like he had all the time in the world to worship and devour my body inch by inch.

"Im... I want to be inside you."

Our gazes locked, the heat between our bodies searing in his gaze and I nodded, lifting my hips and taking his length in my hand.

"Wait..."

He tried to reach for the drawer in his nightstand, but his injuries stopped him. I took over, pulling a condom from the drawer and tearing it open.

"I'm clean," he said, trying to read the expression on my face as I rolled it on him. "But I want you to trust me enough to know that it's true before we go without."

I did trust him. Yes, he'd been with a lot of women, but after what I learned about him tonight, I knew he'd never lie to me and tell me he was safe if he wasn't.

Only I didn't know how to voice any of that, so instead I just nodded.

His grip tightened on my hips as I slowly lowered myself on him, filling me until I was fully seated against him, and he hissed in pleasure.

"Fuck... me. I'll never get over how good you feel," Bant said, one hand leaving my waist to palm my breast again.

I smiled down at him, pressing my hands to his hard chest, rocking my hips against him. My breath hitched at the feel of him inside me and his warm hands all over my skin.

He tried to move, lifting his hips to rock with me but he swore at the pain.

I leaned down, nipping at his ear with my teeth. "You just lie there and let me do the work. I thought the offer was to ride you, remember?"

He chuckled and I sucked his lobe into my mouth, biting down on it.

His eyes closed as I rode him harder, his fingers tightening at my waist. Little sparks of pleasure ignited inside me and I moved faster, my pace matching our now panting breaths.

"Oh my god, Bant..."

The friction between our bodies pushed me higher and higher until I was teetering on the edge, his groans of pleasure pushing me closer.

"Hell yes, Im, ride me hard."

I clenched around him, the pleasure in my core tightening so much I was seconds away from exploding. His hand reached up, fingers pinching my nipple and heat burst through me. I cried out his name, every muscle in my body tightening but I didn't slow the pace of my hips, riding him until he joined me.

"Fuck, Imogen..."

His body contracted as he came, the strong muscles tightening over his perfectly toned body. It was a sight and one I relished bringing out of him.

We both panted through our comedown, my body collapsing on his. He wrapped his strong arms around me, my chest heaving against him.

"That was so good," I said, my voice breathy in post-sex bliss.

He stroked my hair, kissing the top of my head.

"That was better than good. That was the best damn ride I've ever had."

TWENTY

BANT

IMOGEN and I stared into each other's eyes, the sound of a woman moaning coming from her phone on the couch between us.

She pressed her lips together, trying to stifle a laugh. Watching her fight it made my mouth twitch and I clenched my jaw to stop a grin spreading across my face.

A smutty audiobook blared from the speaker, the woman moaning again.

"Don't break," Imogen taunted, taking a sip of her drink.

I did the same, trying not to wince at the heavy-handed pour she'd used when making us vodka and Sprites. It was mostly vodka with a dash of soda, not the other way around.

"You're warning me about breaking? You've lost it three times already. I don't think that hot little body of yours can handle having to down another drink in one go."

My mind flashed back to an hour ago and the insane sex we'd had. My injuries had forced us to go slow, something I don't think I'd ever done with a girl. While I loved to fuck as much as the next guy, the lingering touches and searing kisses had imprinted on my body, making me half hard purely from the memory. It had been hot and, injured or not, I wanted her again.

Instead, we were getting drunk and listening to fictional people get it on.

Lucky jerks.

"What the hell kind of plot is this?"

Imogen bit her lip. "Well, you see, there's a bit of breeding kink mixed with a lactation kink."

I screwed up my face. "Come again?"

"Lactation kink," she repeated as though that explained it.

So far in the book, the woman was getting it on with the dude who'd knocked her up after a one-night stand. They'd decided to live together to raise the kid and their throbbing sexual tension had just reached its peak, with her riding the guy with the moaning soundtrack of a porn star.

"I'm not one to kink shame anyone, power to them I guess."

I raised my drink in Imogen's direction and took a sip just as the woman squirted breast milk all over the guy as she rode him. My drink sprayed from my mouth, the guy groaning through the phone like all his Christmases had come at once.

"What the fuck...?"

Imogen clapped in celebration. "Drink up, playboy. You broke first!"

"Come on! You chose this book on purpose. You knew she was going to give him a titty milk shower, didn't you?"

She grinned back at me. "Maybe..."

I scowled, lifting my glass to my mouth and downing the entire thing.

After four of these, we were both pretty buzzed.

"You know, this night may have started out bad, but you being here has turned it around." I reached out to tuck her hair behind her ear. "Thank you."

She smiled back at me, genuine affection in her eyes. "There's nowhere I'd rather be right now."

I worked to keep the surprise from my face at her response.

They were some of the sweetest words she'd ever said to me. I'd never seen her so relaxed and at ease and it lit me up inside that I'd been able to get her to that place. Imogen was always so serious and controlled. Even when she was having a good time, her keen eye was constantly assessing the people around her. She was smart — psychology suited her. She clearly had an interest in people and what made them tick. But I was most interested in what made her tick and how I could get her to open up to me.

I raised a brow. "Did you just say something nice to me?"

"I've said plenty of nice things to you tonight."

"What have I done to suddenly deserve it? Don't tell me you might actually like me?"

Her expression turned serious. "I always liked you, I just wasn't willing to admit it because I didn't really know you, which meant I didn't know how to trust you. But I learned things about you tonight, about who you really are..." She shrugged. "I like that guy a lot."

Pride flowed through me and I leaned in, sliding a hand along her jaw to tangle in her hair and tugging her mouth to mine. She opened for me, her tongue sliding over mine, my cock stirring in my shorts.

No girl had ever affected me the way Imogen did.

One look, one touch, one taste of her, and I was hooked.

———

TWO HOURS LATER, we were both well on the way to drunk, having ditched the audiobook for music. Taylor Swift was currently blaring from the living room speakers.

"How did I let you convince me to put this on?" I shouted over Taylor singing about some dude from London.

Imogen pulled a face. "You sure know a lot of the lyrics for someone pretending he can't stand her music." She poked me in the cheek. "Admit it, you're a closet Swiftie."

I snorted a laugh, ready to deny it when she gripped my t-shirt, tugging me towards her. "There's nothing hotter than a man who likes Taylor Swift."

Before I could respond, she covered her mouth with mine and my dick was half hard in an instant.

I reached for her, wincing when my ribs twinged but pushing it aside to haul her into my lap. Her knees fell on either side of my waist and her hands gripped my face as she devoured my mouth.

Fuck me... it was so hot.

I had no idea if it was the alcohol or the connection we'd made tonight, but something had her letting her walls down and I prayed to God it stayed that way. I'd waited a long time for her to let me in, now that she had, I never wanted to be shut out again.

She pulled back with a contented smile. "Do you have any tattoos? I haven't seen any and I've seen most of you at this point."

I smirked. Yes, she had.

"No, do you?"

She shook her head, tilting it to the side while she thought about it. "But I think I've always wanted one."

"You think?"

She nodded and I smacked my hands against her thighs. "Well, then, let's go to Jeri's room."

Her brow pinched. "Is this some kind of weird fantasy of yours? To get it on in your teammates room?"

I let out a laugh. "Absolutely not, who knows what the hell goes on in there. I want to show you something."

"Is it his sex toy collection? Because I like Jericho and all, but I really don't need to see that."

"Will you just trust me?"

She climbed off me. "Only if you're forcing me to."

She took both my hands to help me to my feet, then put my arm around her shoulders to prop me up. Her own arm went to my waist, determined to help me walk down the hall.

There was no way in hell I was actually going to lean my weight on her and use her as a human crutch, but I appreciated the support and the bodily contact. I'd take any excuse to have her pressed against me.

We made it to Jericho's room and I flung the door open, heading for his desk to find what I was looking for.

"What on earth is that?" Imogen asked.

"A tattoo machine."

Her eyes widened. "You're joking. Why does Jericho have that?"

"He decided freshman year that he wanted to learn. He took a course online and convinced half the guys on the team to let him practice on them."

She stared at the machine. "Did you let him practice on you?"

I pulled a face. "Hell no, you should see some of the shit

the guys have tattooed on them. Jeri may know how to nail a free throw every time but he's terrible at tattoos."

She laughed. "I actually want to see them now."

I nodded at the machine. "So, are you up for it?"

"Up for what? Letting you tattoo me?" She stared at me like I'd grown three heads. "Do you even know how?"

"Jeri has shown me once or twice. And I've seen him do it a bunch of times."

"Wow, I feel so reassured." She perched on the edge of Jericho's desk, gripping it to steady herself. "I don't even know what I'd get."

I held up a hand to get her to wait a second, limping back to the living room to get my phone, then coming back to show her a picture, a grin spreading across my face.

She stared at it, a laugh bursting out of her.

"Yeah, okay. Let's do it."

I STUMBLED down the stairs the next morning, swearing the whole way over my fucking ribs.

Jesus, they hurt more today than they had yesterday.

The endless vodka and sodas Imogen and I had downed definitely helped me forget. As well as her smoking hot body wrapped around me all night.

She'd woken early this morning to head home. I smiled, my hazy hungover mind conjuring a vague image of her leaning over the bed to kiss me goodbye before she left.

Last night at the shelter had sucked. But things had improved exponentially the minute Imogen had turned up on my doorstep.

I hadn't missed the rage and hurt marring her beautiful face when I'd opened the door after cancelling our date. I hated that I'd put it there by standing her up at the diner. But she'd shifted the moment she laid eyes on me, switching to nurse mode. And her particular brand of healing was one I was more than willing to get onboard with.

Shuffling into the kitchen, I parked my ass on a stool at the counter and dropped my head in my hands, groaning.

"Big night last night, sweetheart?" Hernandez grinned around a glass of orange juice.

"You could say that. Got into a fight, then got drunk."

I looked up in time to see Davis and Hernandez shoot each other a surprised glance, Hooker chuckling from his spot over by the toaster.

"You got into a fight?" Davis said.

"Shelter."

His eyes widened. "Oh, damn."

"Is Coach going to be pissed or can you play?"

I shrugged. "I can't play today, that's for sure. I'll go talk to him, try to explain."

"Good luck with that," Hooker said, snatching his toast from the toaster and taking a seat at the counter beside me.

I groaned again, running my hands through my hair and wincing, only this time it wasn't my ribs.

"Fuck. Why does my finger hurt like a mother fu...?" I stared down at it. "Oh shit."

Davis shot me a look. "What? You get it caught on a sorority girl's bra and break a nail?"

I scrubbed my good hand over my face. "I gave myself a tattoo."

My teammates stared back at me.

"I knew someone had been in my room last night," Jericho said, strolling into the kitchen and heading for the fridge. Good thing he wasn't territorial about his space.

"You gave yourself a tattoo?" Hooker asked, all of them leaning over the counter to see it.

I held up my index finger, showing off the curved half circle line that made up the world's most out of context ink of all time.

"Wow, dude, not sure I'd call that a tattoo," Hooker said, chuckling.

"How drunk were you last night?" Hernandez asked.

"Not that drunk."

Although my pounding head would disagree.

"Well, when people ask, tell them you were off your face," Davis offered. "That's the only way to explain that embarrassing thing on your finger."

Of course it looked stupid. It didn't make any sense when it was missing the other half.

But I wasn't about to tell my teammates it was on Imogen's finger.

TWENTY-ONE

IMOGEN

...

BANT: Hernandez was stoked you chose to wear his jersey to the game tonight.

IMOGEN: I'm just out here making people's dreams come true.

BANT: How about making mine come true?

IMOGEN: Pretty sure I make your dreams come true every time I get naked for you.

BANT: I take it back, wear whatever fucking jersey you want, so long as you keep getting naked for me.

IMOGEN: That's what I thought.

BANT SLUNG an arm around my shoulders, toying with the buttons on my coat.

"You know you don't have to meet me after class every day, right? I am capable of walking places on my own."

My tone was teasing, like I thought Bant was being

totally clingy by meeting me most days to walk me home, but I secretly loved it. If there were times he got caught up at practice or had to head to the shelter, I found I was disappointed when I emerged from whatever class I'd been in and he wasn't standing there looking like a sporty snack I couldn't wait to unwrap.

His arm tightened around my neck and he pressed a kiss to my temple. "You love it. And I know you well enough now to know the prickly cactus routine you put on is an act. Deep down you're actually a marshmallow who loves to be cuddled."

"Cuddle a lot of marshmallows do you, big guy?"

He grinned down at me. "You know what I mean. You want people to think you're strong and impenetrable, and you are." He dipped his head, kissing my cheek. "But you're also soft." He moved to brush his lips over the other cheek as we walked and I turned my head to assist. "And sweet." Then his mouth dipped to my throat. "And obsessed with me."

I laughed, shoving him away and he stumbled a step, chuckling.

"You're the one who's obsessed, playboy."

He took my hand, reeling me back in. "Damn right I am."

His mouth moved for mine but we were interrupted by someone calling his name.

A petite girl with long blonde hair, assessing brown eyes and a perfect body walked towards us, smiling at Bant. He stiffened beside me, his expression instantly shuttering. He threw his arm around my shoulder once more, only this time his body was rigid when he tucked me to his side. His light-hearted mood from only a moment ago evaporated, like he'd shut down the second he'd spotted her.

Who is this girl?

She came to a stop in front of us, not even acknowledging my presence, eyes only for Bant. "Hi stranger, it's been a while."

"Delaney."

There wasn't an ounce of his usual warmth to his tone, and I glanced up at him in surprise. Surly was a new look for him.

"I've been coming to your games again. You've been killing it on the court this season."

Bant grunted a response and gave her nothing else. The usual charismatic charmer was long gone.

"How's Tanner?" Bant asked, staring back at her with hard eyes.

If she noticed his hard edges, she didn't show it, tilting her head to the side. "Same as he's always been. I don't see him as much as I used to though."

She stared up at Bant, waiting for him to react. When he didn't, her gaze turned calculating as she looked him over, as though he were a new prospect she was considering.

I hated it instantly.

I thrust my hand towards her. "Hi, I'm Imogen."

Her attention flicked to me and she smiled, not unkindly, shaking my hand.

"Delaney Parker."

Bant's arm tightened around my neck. "We need to get going, but it was fun running into you, Del."

He didn't give her a chance to respond, shepherding us away.

When we were out of earshot, I peered up at him. "Who was that?"

I tried to sound casual and keep the raging curiosity from my voice.

He shrugged. "Just a girl I used to know."

"You used to know a lot of girls, I've never seen you react like that to any of them."

He stopped in the path, dropping his mouth to mine in a searing kiss.

"Right now, I only want to know one girl. Intimately."

He gave me a pointed look.

"Well, in that case," I said, smiling up at him. "Your place or mine?"

MUSIC POUNDED THROUGH THE FLOOR, the whole room vibrating with the sound. The crush of bodies in the living room of the frat house was one writhing sweaty mess, but I was loving every second of it.

Stella, Monty and I danced together, downing luke-warm cups of beer, our voices hoarse from shouting out song lyrics like the drunk college girls we were.

It was an ABC party at one of the frats — Anything But Clothes.

Stella had strung together a minidress made entirely out of red cups, while Monty had made a dress out of a Twister mat. I'd gone for a minidress made out of ivy that had been a bitch to get into it. The only way I was getting out of it at the end of the night was if someone cut me out. I looked good though.

"I need a refill," Stella called over the music, motioning to her cup.

Monty and I smiled. Stella was always a slow starter when it came to drinking on a night out, but once she was three drinks deep there was no stopping her.

She spotted someone from her art workshop, turning to

hug her with a squeal, and the two of them fell into shouted conversation.

"Let's hit the keg in the kitchen," I said to Monty, collecting Stella's cup and threading through the crowd, Monty at my heels.

The frat bros manning the keg were all too happy to oblige us when we thrust our cups in their direction. I glanced around the room, a commotion by the back door drawing my attention.

A bunch of the basketball and lacrosse guys were entertaining a group of girls with stories about the pranks the two teams loved to play on each other, each player more loud and animated than the last.

Bant was among them, shirtless, wearing shorts made out of boxes of Bud Lite, complete with a hammer made from the same, the overall look akin to some kind of ripped, beer-sponsored superhero.

He looked hot as hell and I had to stop myself from marching across the room and running my tongue all over him in some desperate bid to claim him.

He isn't mine to claim.

One of the girls sidled closer, sliding her arms around his waist. I bit the inside of my cheek, hating the feeling that flared inside me at the sight. Bant wasn't my boyfriend, he could cozy up to whoever he liked.

Instead, he threw his hands up in the air in an effort to avoid touching her. "I can't, I'm a taken man!" he repeated over and over, shaking his head and trying to back away.

The brunette clung to his waist, giggling, until he gripped her wrists and removed her arms.

"Since when does Luke Bantempelli have a girlfriend? I thought he didn't do relationships," a sophomore nearby muttered to the girl next to her.

The girl shrugged. "That's what he told my friend from my econ class when they hooked up last year."

Monty quirked a brow at me, her voice low so only I could hear. "You wouldn't know anything about that would you, Imogen?"

It had taken Stella about eight-point-seven seconds to tell Monty about Bant and I after the night she busted me sneaking him in at one am. The two of them had been dining out on it ever since, giving me an endlessly hard time about how much I'd always claimed to hate him.

Whoever said it's a thin line between love and hate was on to something.

Not that what I felt for Bant was even close to love. No way. It was pure lust and a definite addiction to his monster dick.

"Nope. I wouldn't know a thing about it."

I was careful to mask my expression. No one needed to know just how much I was swooning over the fact that Bant had pushed that girl away.

No good would come of that at all.

AN HOUR later I was standing in the hallway, talking to a hot frat bro who'd cornered me on my way back to Stella.

He was no cocky ball player with abs you could grate parmesan cheese on, but he was cute enough and his attention was the perfect ego boost. It's not like I'd worn this outfit so guys *wouldn't* notice me.

Without warning, a heavy arm landed over my shoulders, Bant grinning at the guy across from me.

"Who's your friend, Im? You going to introduce me?"

I gave the guy an awkward smile, glancing sideways at Bant. "I don't know his name yet, we just met."

Bant's grin widened. "New friends? I love making those." He thrust his spare hand at the guy, the other still around my neck in a clear marking of territory. "Luke Bantempelli."

The guy looked a little uneasy as he shook his hand. "Tom Hanson."

"Pleasure to meet you, Tom. Welcome to the party. I assume you've been here before? This frat throws some killer parties. Though not as good as the ones we throw at the basketball house. You know what I mean, Tom?"

With the forced edge to Bant's smile and the way his arm tightened around me, anyone would think he was jealous.

Tom glanced between me and Bant. "Uh... yeah, sure. Great parties all round."

"Great place to meet people," Bant went on. "I'm sure my girl has some single friends she can introduce you to."

He was absolutely jealous. He may as well tear off his Bud Lite shorts and pee in a circle around me with the neanderthal way he was trying to claim me.

"No need," Tom said with a forced smile. "I need a refill, so I'll catch you later."

Bant's smile widened. "Great meeting you, Tom."

Tom gave him an uneasy nod without so much as a backwards glance in my direction before he disappeared into the party.

I rounded on Bant. "Your girl? And I have some single friends I can introduce him to?"

"What?" he asked, suddenly all innocence.

"I'm not your girl, you can't just claim me because you're jealous I'm talking to some guy."

He scoffed. "Jealous? Please. What do I have to be jealous of that guy for? Have you seen me?" He motioned to his bare abs.

I rolled my eyes. "They're okay. I've seen better."

A total lie.

His expression filled with mock outrage and he crowded me against the wall. "Seen better? Better doesn't exist, Im, and you know it." He slapped a hand against his stomach between us. "You love these bad boys."

He had a point. His body was near impossible to resist. But there was no way in hell I was going to admit that to him.

"Should I be worried about your girlfriend getting jealous and coming over to scratch my eyes out?" I asked, quirking a brow.

He frowned. "What girlfriend?"

"This girl you're apparently taken by."

He smirked. "Ah, you saw that? See the things I do for you? I rebuff every other woman because you're all I need." He reached for me, wrapping a hand around my hip and tugging my hips to his. "You look so damn hot tonight, I've never been so into horticulture." His eyes roamed my body. "All I can think about is getting you alone so I can make you moan my name."

I swallowed, clinging to his shoulders to steady me.

"Is that so?"

He nodded like an eager puppy, his blue eyes shining.

"Then I guess I could be persuaded to let you."

TWENTY-TWO

BANT

I PULLED my phone from my bag as I exited the locker room after our game, distracted as I walked back out on the court. We'd absolutely smoked Ohio in a thirty-eight-point steam roll, which meant I should be celebrating with my teammates. Only when I glanced at my phone, I had two missed calls and a text from Raven.

RAVEN: *Renee and Kelsie are leaving. Kelsie's asking after you.*

"Shit."

I stopped walking and stared at words on the screen.

They'd found a new shelter? I wasn't ready to say good-bye, but this wasn't about me. Moving shelters was what was best for Renee and Kelsie; it would keep them safe. But there was no way Kelsie would ever forgive me if I wasn't there when they left.

Raven had sent the message more than an hour ago, which meant there was a chance I'd already missed them.

My stomach dropped at the thought. I had to get to the shelter fast and pray like hell I could catch them. But Davis had driven me to the game tonight and he'd already left after telling me to catch a ride home with one of the guys.

I glanced around the court, looking for anyone who could drive me to the shelter.

Imogen was at the far end, talking to some dude with glasses wearing a Pierson fan jersey that he didn't have the physique to fill. I shoved aside my momentary burst of jealousy at him holding any of her attention and jogged over.

"Hey Im, did you drive here tonight?"

She glanced at me, whatever sarcastic remark she'd been about to snap back with dying on her lips when she took in my desperate expression.

"Yes."

"Can you give me a ride to the shelter? I wouldn't ask if it wasn't important."

She pulled her keys from her purse. "Yeah, of course."

I turned and headed for the door to the parking lot, a small sense of satisfaction filling me when she jogged after me, not even bothering to say goodbye to the nerdy dude in the jersey.

"Is everything okay? What's going on?"

"You know that mom and daughter I told you about at the shelter? They're leaving. I have to get there in time to say goodbye, they're too important to me."

We piled into the car, Imogen cutting off anyone she had to in order to make it out of the parking lot fast, and we arrived at the shelter within ten minutes.

Raven was the first person I ran into as we hustled through the back door.

"Thank God you made it. Kelsie would have lost it if she didn't get to see you before they left."

I gripped her arms. "Thank you for texting me. I owe you, Raven."

She smiled, nodding, as I headed into the dining room, Imogen close behind. I jogged through the hallways, hoping like hell I wasn't too late.

When I came to a stop in the foyer, Renee and Kelsie were standing with Marie and Hadiza, the shelter directors, with suitcases at their feet.

"Luke!"

Kelsie's face lit up the moment she saw me and she bolted in my direction. I crouched down, my arms wide and she threw herself into them so hard we almost toppled backwards.

"I can't believe you weren't going to say goodbye," Kelsie said in her small voice.

I had to choke down the emotion suddenly clogging my throat. I'd been so desperate to get here in time, I hadn't thought about what this moment might actually be like once I did. She was only a kid, but Kelsie was the best part of my week. The way her little face lit up every time I turned up at the shelter was everything. There was a real possibility this would be the last time I'd ever see her.

My arms tightened around her. "Not a chance kid, you're my best gal."

Kelsie pulled back, glancing up at Imogen.

"Don't say it too loud, your girlfriend will get jealous," she stage-whispered.

I glanced over my shoulder at Imogen, who smiled down at Kelsie with genuine affection.

"Don't worry, she knows she comes second to my best girl," I whispered back.

Imogen nodded and Kelsie's expression filled with pride. Then her face fell just as fast.

"Mommy and me are leaving. We're going to go stay somewhere else. Will you work at our new home too?"

I took her hand in mine and shook my head. "I won't be there. But your mom will be, and I'm sure there will be a big group of kids just like you to play with."

Kelsie shook her head. "There's nobody like me. Mommy told me that."

I chuckled. "Your mommy is right, Kels. There's nobody like you."

She flung herself at me again, her little arms wrapping around my neck.

"I'll miss you, Luke."

My chest tightened at her words, and I worked to clear my throat. "I'll miss you too, kid."

Out of the corner of my eye, Imogen wiped a tear from her cheek, just as Renee made her way over to us. Kelsie pulled away, wrapping her arms around her mom's leg.

"I can't thank you enough, Luke. For everything." Renee reached for my hand, giving it a squeeze. "You mean so much to so many here. Kelsie and I will never forget you."

I swallowed hard. "You have my number. Use it any time you need anything."

Renee nodded, giving me a small smile.

"He's one of the good ones," she said to Imogen. "You take care of him."

Imogen nodded. "I'll do my best. Good luck."

Renee took Kelsie's hand and the two of them walked back to Marie and Hadiza, who helped them carry their bags to the door.

My chest tightened for the second time, and my eyes burned as I watched them leave.

I could still remember the day my mom and I had

moved out of the shelter for good. We'd left behind so many good people; some my mom was still in touch with. If it hadn't been for them, there was no way my mom would have been able to get back on her feet like she had, which meant there was no way I'd be at Pierson living my dream. I hoped like hell I'd made some small difference in Kelsie's life the same way.

Imogen stepped up beside me, her hand sliding into mine.

"Who knew you were such a softie under all that swagger?"

I smiled. "There's so much more to me than my pretty packaging."

She rolled her eyes. "And he's back. Way to ruin an incredibly sweet moment."

I brought our joined hands to my lips. "Thank you for driving me here so I could do this."

She smiled back at me. "Of course, glad I could help."

TWENTY-THREE

IMOGEN

I CHECKED my phone for the fourth time in the past hour, mentally kicking myself for being *that* girl.

Bant had taken to texting me after class or on his way to practice, usually just to check in or see how my day was going. But the past four days had been radio silence, with the exception of yesterday when he'd sent me a short, late-night message claiming he was swamped with practice and the extra shifts he'd taken on at the shelter and classes, but he'd see me this weekend.

The fact I found myself yet again checking my phone for a message from him made my stomach twist.

Yes, I could message him, but that felt like revealing too much. I couldn't ignore the insecure little voice that had taken up residence in my head that told me Bant had gone quiet because he was losing interest in me and pulling away. I wasn't about to do anything that would make me look like some clingy girl who couldn't read the writing on the wall.

I'd been pulled into these games before with other guys. I'd refused to show my hand and reveal my feelings then, and I wasn't about to do it now.

Remaining aloof, disinterested, unaffected was safer.

You couldn't get hurt if you didn't care, right?

Guys always pursued you hard when they wanted to get you into bed, harder if you didn't make it easy for them. They'd be sweet and attentive when they were getting laid, then a few weeks in, things would cool off. They'd suddenly get busy and before you knew it, they were giving you the brush off. Sometimes it was subtle, other times it was overt. Every time it hurt, and I hated that I'd let myself get in this position again.

Whether Bant was pulling away or not, I hated that I was sitting here questioning it. I was smart and fun and strong, and yet I was spending so much mental energy worrying about whether or not some guy still liked me.

I hated it.

This is why it was so much easier just to cut things off before they went anywhere. Or not get involved at all. It saved a whole lot of heartbreak.

Wasn't it easier to be alone anyway? Hadn't I promised myself I'd be focused on my goals this year?

It was time to buck up and protect my heart. I was done with being played.

"Who kicked your puppy? You look ready to go on a rampage right now," Monty said, sliding into the seat across from me at the table in the Drysdale dining hall.

It was dumpling day, so the place was packed. But Monty, Stella, and I had come up with a system our freshman year — divide and conquer. Hit three different lines and order an extra-large serve of three different kinds of dumplings, then snag the first open table we could find. We'd then stuff our faces in a shared feast.

I loved dumpling day because it meant no matter how busy we got, the three of us would eventually come back together over delicious juicy sacks of steamed meat.

"No one, I'm fine." I placed my phone face down on the table.

Stella dropped into the seat next to me, placing her bowl of dumplings in the middle. "Oh yeah, that was believable. You sound fine."

I took the bowl and chopsticks Monty offered, pouring some soy sauce in the bottom.

"Don't tell me," Monty said, spooning dumplings into her bowl. "Bant's monster D finally poked you in the eye and you're mad."

Despite my best efforts I couldn't help my laugh.

"My eyes remain intact, thank you very much." I sighed. "I don't know, it's whatever. I think it's time I cut it off."

Stella paused in her perusal of the food, frowning at me.

"Really? Every time I've seen you two together he's been totally obsessed with you." She gave me a wry smile. "Particularly if the noises coming from your bedroom are anything to go by."

I swatted at her shoulder, Monty letting out a laugh.

"So, the smooth-talking player who's slept with half the girls on campus is good in bed? Shocker. But I'm over it, it's time to move on."

Monty and Stella shared a look.

"Don't think I don't see the secret conversation you two are having with your eyes," I said, picking up a spicy dumpling and shoving it all in my mouth. "Bant and I were never going to be long term. He doesn't have it in him and

I'm not interested in getting cheated on yet again by some campus Romeo who can't keep it in his pants."

Monty levelled me a flat stare. "Do you really think that's who Bant is?"

"Wasn't it you who regaled me with stories about how he has so many girls on speed dial he can barely remember their names?"

"Yes, but—"

"No buts," I cut her off. "I'm not going to get sucked in by his dicksand and find myself screwed over yet again."

Stella smiled. "Sucking, dicksand, screwed over. So many innuendos in one sentence I don't even know where to start."

Monty pointed her chopsticks in my direction. "There's no denying Bant is an absolute babe though. He's like Kristoff from Frozen, only... hotter."

She scooped a dumpling into her mouth, making blissed-out noises as she chewed.

"Not possible," I said, doing the same. "Kristoff is a dreamboat."

Stella nodded. "But Bant is too. The boy is a walking, talking sexual invitation. He can't help it."

I glanced between the two of them. "You both remember you have boyfriends, right? No need to drool over their best friend."

Monty snorted a laugh. "Yeah, I have a boyfriend, but I also have eyes. Bant's as hot as they come, don't act like you don't love it."

I went to reply when a figure loomed over me, knocking a fist against the table like he was knocking on a door.

"Ladies," Jackson said with a cocky grin, folding his arms across his chest and staring down at me like I was a dumpling he wanted to dip in soy sauce and suck dry.

"Jackson." I shoved another dumpling in my mouth, forcing out a smile as I chewed.

He leaned down, hands planted on the table.

"I'm stopping by to see if you've changed your mind about letting me take you out to dinner. We both know you've knocked me back before, but I've been a hard-core beast on the lacrosse field lately, and I know how much that dominance turns you ladies on."

He grinned at each of us in turn.

Monty pulled a face, reaching for another dumpling. "Wow, Im, how could you possibly say no to an offer like that?"

Only... I was contemplating it.

Yes, Jackson was arrogant. But show me a guy on a successful sports team who wasn't. We were friends with the basketball players and they all loved their own reflections more than anything else. Maybe there was a chance Jackson was different one on one. Maybe when no one else was around, the showboating bullshit dropped away to reveal a secretly sweet heart of gold inside him?

Or maybe I was looking for any excuse to push Bant out of my mind and my bed and Jackson was the perfect way to do it.

It's not like Bant was my boyfriend. We hadn't ever spoken about being exclusive. We were fuck buddies at best. For all I knew he was sleeping with at least three other girls right now, which meant going to dinner with Jackson wasn't a big deal.

"Sure, why not?"

Monty choked on her dumpling, Stella reaching across the table to thump her on the back.

Jackson slid his phone in front of me. "Hit me with your digits."

Hopefully phrases like that would also disappear from his vocabulary when we're alone.

I added my number to his phone and handed it back. He winked down at me and sauntered back to his friends.

"Imogen, you can't be serious," Stella said, her brow pinched in disbelief.

"What? He's cute."

Monty pulled a face. "He's obnoxious. He's got arrogance sweating out of his pores."

I tilted my head at her. "I'm sorry, but isn't that your usual type given who you're dating?"

She smirked. West Wright had been one of the cockiest guys on campus when he'd been at Pierson U. At least until Monty.

"West's arrogance was charming," Stella offered. "That guy makes me want to face palm him five different ways just for opening his mouth."

Monty dipped her dumpling in soy sauce, waving it in my direction while she spoke. "He has big refuses-to-go-down-on-his-girlfriend energy. Do you really want to date a guy like that? No good will come of it."

"You certainly won't." Stella laughed, and I pulled a face.

There was no way I was going to admit that until today I'd felt exactly the same way about Jackson. But he was cute and he was keen, not to mention the perfect distraction from a suddenly near-silent Bant. I wouldn't be the loser sitting home alone waiting for his call, while he was probably seeing multiple girls.

I shoved aside the voice in my head telling me I was self-sabotaging because I was scared. It was normal to be afraid of getting your heart shattered, wasn't it? This wasn't self-sabotage. It was self-preservation. Better to be the player than to be played... *right*?

My phone vibrated on the table and I turned it over.

"Your mom again?" Stella asked.

I nodded. "I better take this."

Pushing to my feet, I made my way to the door, sitting on a bench inside the lobby. "Hey Mom."

"Sweetheart, it's so good to finally hear your voice. I've been calling you for weeks and you never answer."

Guilt overwhelmed me. I'd never dodged my mom's calls the way I had the past few weeks, but I just didn't know how to deal with everything that was going on at home right now. I'd committed to being there for Lola, who texted me regular updates about the war our parents were waging in our formerly peaceful family home, but speaking to my mom would make it all too real.

It had been cruel to avoid her though. If something bad was going down with my dad, she needed me to be there for her.

"Sorry, it's been crazy busy here. I can talk now, is everything okay?"

The line was silent, then my mom blew out a long breath.

"Your father and I are having some issues."

I nodded even though she couldn't see it. "Lola mentioned things have been tense. Anything I can do?"

"No, thank you, sweetheart. I just wanted you to hear the truth before things got any more out of hand."

Dread pooled in my stomach. I was almost certain I didn't want to know the truth, but mom wanted to tell me and short of hanging up on her, I was going to hear it.

"Your father was unfaithful with his assistant while on a work trip in Chicago."

Silence descended, and I struggled to find the right thing to say. So many emotions swirled inside me. Shock that my dad would do something like that, furious that he'd treat my mom that way, the sharp sting of betrayal at him ruining our family.

Also, a little surprised my mom had told me, if I was honest.

Do all men cheat?

I'd always looked up to my dad. Held him up as the standard of man my future husband would have to aspire to. Now he was a cheating asshole just like all the others. If my own father couldn't be trusted to stay faithful within his marriage, what hope did I have of finding a guy I could give my heart to and believe he'd take care of it?

"I'm so sorry, Mom."

"It's been a tough time. I don't know if I can forgive him, Imogen."

"I don't blame you. I don't know if I can forgive him either."

There was shuffling on the other end of the line and Mom sniffled, blowing her nose.

"He's your father. I don't want you to let this come between you. He cheated on me, not you and your sisters. But I wanted you to know given there's a chance he may not live here anymore."

The dumplings in my stomach turned to stones. My family was breaking up. Not that I blamed my mom; if it were me, I'd have already sent him packing.

You like your assistant so much, Dad, go live with her.

Tears burned the backs of my eyes, desperate to fall, but I wouldn't fall apart on the phone to my mom. I should be comforting her right now, not the other way around.

I spent the next fifteen minutes doing just that, until

Monty and Stella appeared in front of me, my book bag and a takeout container of dumplings in Stella's hands.

There was no way I could eat right now.

"Mom, I'm so sorry but I have to go. My next class starts in five minutes."

"Oh, of course, you get going. We can talk some more later. I just want you to know how much I love you, sweetheart."

"I love you too, Mom."

We hung up and I stared at my phone screen in disbelief.

My father had cheated on my mother. Their picture-perfect marriage had been a lie. And men were clearly incapable of ever staying faithful.

A lump formed in my throat, threatening to choke me. How was this my life right now?

Monty and Stella dropped down on the bench on either side of me.

"Im, what happened?"

"My dad cheated on my mom."

Monty's mouth dropped open. "No fucking way."

Monty and I were childhood friends from back home. She'd known my parents since we were kids. None of what was happening between them made any sense.

"I should go," I said, getting to my feet and taking my bag from Stella.

"You sure you don't want to blow off classes and talk about this?"

I shook my head. "No, thanks, though. I think I need to walk around for a bit."

They both pushed to their feet, hugging me, but I felt totally numb.

My world was on the verge of breaking. I could feel it. And I had no idea how to stop it.

I left my friends, hurrying down the front steps of the building and walking across campus. The cold wind bit at my cheeks, but I barely felt it. All I could feel was the hurt and betrayal at my family falling apart.

I'd told Monty and Stella I wanted to be alone but there was one person I wanted to see. I wanted to be wrapped up in his strong arms while he told me everything was going to be okay. Or failing that, I wanted to get naked with him to help me forget.

Unlocking my phone, I dialed Bant's number. I bit the inside of my cheek, listening to it ring.

And ring and ring and ring, never picking up. I ended the call, sliding my phone in the pocket of my coat, and kept walking.

Was he busy with classes or the shelter? Or had he screened my call?

Or worse... was he with someone else right now? Maybe he'd glanced at his phone and seen my name, tossing it aside to get it on with some hot girl who didn't have a mountain of baggage, which now included some newly added daddy issues.

Regret flooded me. He wasn't my boyfriend. I shouldn't have tried to turn to him for emotional support.

My life may be falling apart, but that didn't mean I had to. I took a deep breath, pushing my shoulders back, my sadness hardening into anger.

At my father for cheating on my mother and ruining our family.

At Bant for going missing when I needed him the most.

But mostly I was mad at myself.

For letting a boy into my heart when I knew better.

TWENTY-FOUR

BANT

GRUNTING, I hoisted the weight bar over my head and dropped it into the rack, shaking out my hand where I'd knocked the tattoo on my finger, a twinge of pain radiating there.

"Nice set, bro," Davis said, slapping my shoulder from where he'd been spotting me. "Shame that stupid ass tattoo got in your way."

I huffed a laugh, sitting up and reaching for my towel to wipe the sweat from my face and shoulders.

Coach had been riding us extra hard the past couple of weeks—scheduling extra practices, demanding extra sessions in the weight room. Every second that wasn't spent in class or dedicated to basketball, I'd been spending at the shelter. They were shorter than ever on volunteers yet every bed was full, so I'd been putting in extra time in the kitchens to help Raven feed everyone.

I barely found time to sleep, let alone party or socialize.

I hadn't managed to find time to see Imogen either. Most nights I was so wiped that by the time I got home I showered and fell into bed. But Imogen was never far from my mind, and I couldn't wait to get her alone this weekend.

"Let's swap out," I said to Davis, standing from the bench and letting him take my place.

Hernandez grunted on the bench beside us, his bar clanging back into the rack, narrowly missing Li's fingers where he was spotting him.

"Boys, boys, boys," a voice boomed through the room. "No need to make so much racket just because your spindly basketball arms can't hack some real weight."

All eyes turned at the slight, ready to rip the guy a new one, until we realized it was Carlsen Cooper, the lacrosse captain and the nicest dude on campus.

"Because lacrosse players are known for their buff physiques," Davis cut back.

"Nah, we're known for our killer plays on the field *and* in the sack," Jackson said, strolling into the room behind Coop.

I crossed my arms over my chest and worked to fight my annoyance. Jackson was the worst kind of cocky for someone who wasn't even the best player on his team. The fact Monty told me he'd been trying to harass Imogen into a date for months made me hate the guy even more. Seemed the time I'd intervened hadn't been his first attempt.

"You guys are here late," Coop said, surveying the room. "Your coach riding your asses as much as ours is?"

I nodded. "Dude has a boner about winning this year. Being more of a hard ass than ever."

Davis snorted beside me. "Doesn't help when you piss him off by getting caught with a girl in the locker room showers."

Coop's laugh filled the weight room. "Same old Bantempelli."

"Nice one, bro." Jackson offered me his fist to pound.

I glanced down at it, leaving him hanging. There was no way I was going to let him congratulate me on hooking up with any girl, but definitely not when that girl was Imogen.

"You two come to shoot the shit or you need us for something?" Davis asked.

Coop's face lit with a grin. "Came to invite you to the frat house for a little beer and video game action tomorrow night."

I glanced between the two lacrosse players. I liked Coop and ordinarily wouldn't hesitate at an invitation from him, but I could live without spending what little downtime I had right now with a tool like Jackson Marin. Besides, I'd been hoping to snag some alone time with Imogen tomorrow night, which was a way more appealing offer.

Reading my rejection before I'd even voiced it, Coop gripped Jackson by the shoulders, giving him a friendly shake.

"Don't worry, this joker won't be there. He's got a hot date."

"Oh yeah?" Davis piped up. "You finally get Carlsen's mom to agree to be seen with you outside her bedroom?"

Coop gave Davis a swift punch to the shoulder, grinning. "Watch it, my mama is an angel. She would never go near a jackass like Marin."

Jackson crossed his arms like he was king dick. "Finally got Imogen Knight to agree to go out with me."

I stilled, my jaw clenching so tight I was likely to bust a blood vessel.

Surely, I'd heard him wrong. There was no way Imogen

would agree to date this tool, not with everything going on between us. Not to mention she couldn't stand the guy.

There was a time when she couldn't stand you either.

I ignored the voice in my head. Things had changed between us the night after the shelter. We'd become closer than ever. So why the fuck was she going out with this asshole?

"Errrr... how'd you manage that?" Davis shot me a glance, clearly worried I was going to injure myself with the way I was grinding my teeth. Or maybe injure Jackson.

"Wore her down with the Marin charm obviously. The ladies love it."

He was so goddamn smug, I wanted to pummel him to the floor.

"I hope we're cool, bro." Jackson nodded in my direction, oblivious. "You said she was your girl a few months ago, but Coop said you don't usually keep them around much longer than that."

Ordinarily Coop would be right, but Imogen was different. She wasn't just some girl I was sleeping with. She was *the* girl. The one who changed everything. And the thought of this smug fool or any others like him getting anywhere near her made me want to break something. Maybe a whole lot of somethings.

"Sure, bro. We're cool."

My sarcasm and the seething rage inside me clearly went right over the guy's head because he slapped my shoulder like we were buds.

"Alright, well, I'll catch you two tomorrow night," Coop called, heading for the door and taking Jackson with him.

Davis turned to me as soon as they were gone. "Shit, I know that look."

I leaned against the weight rack, dropping my head and

gripping the bar until my knuckles turned white. "Why the hell would she accept a date with him?"

I caught Davis's shrug in the mirrors. "Maybe you should talk to her about it."

That was a sure-fire way to scare Imogen off. She was like a spooked horse. One hint of a commitment conversation and she was likely to bolt. Although she probably thought the same about me. Only it wasn't commitment I was afraid of, it was getting hurt.

My mom always said I loved hard, but that had come back to bite me in the ass in the worst possible way with Delaney. I'd loved her and she'd betrayed me. After that, I'd shut down and refused to feel anything for anyone again. If I didn't let anyone get close to me, I wouldn't get hurt. As a college ball player, I was expected to be a womanizer not a one-woman guy, so somewhere along the line I'd learned to play into the stereotype and shut off my feelings at the same time.

But if I were honest, I'd never wanted that. All I really wanted was someone to love, who loved me back, no questions asked. I'd convinced myself that girl didn't exist for me, at least not at college. So instead of committing to a relationship, I'd committed to having fun with whoever came along.

Until Imogen.

Who, despite the super-hot hook-ups and the connection I knew we'd been forming these past few weeks, had accepted a date with the biggest jackass on the lacrosse team.

Which meant I'd gone and done exactly what I promised myself I never would again.

I'd let someone in and now I was totally and utterly screwed.

I SHOVED my hands in my jacket pockets, walking along the dark path toward the library.

I'd hit the showers after the weight room, trying to scrub away the rage and, if I was totally honest, the hurt at learning Imogen was going out with that asshole Marin. As soon as I was done, I'd sent her a text asking if she was around and she'd replied saying she was studying at the library. When I reached the steps to the oldest building on campus, she was already waiting for me.

"Hey," she said quietly, her expression unreadable.

What the hell had happened? Yeah, I'd been busier than usual, but surely she knew it wasn't about her. It didn't change how I felt about her and how much I wanted to be around her. If it were my choice, I'd blow off classes and basketball and spend every damn second with her. But I also knew if I told her any of that, she'd spook and bolt in the other direction faster than I could blink. I'd let myself get caught up in Delaney like that and it had damn near ruined me.

I stared at Imogen, taking her in. She was the hottest girl I'd ever laid eyes on, even when she was scowling at me, which was pretty much always. She was strong and sweet at the same time, and so fucking fierce it took my damn breath away.

Right now, though, she could barely look me in the eye.

"I saw Jackson today."

Her gaze snapped to mine and what looked a lot like regret flashed in her eyes before she masked it.

"He had some interesting things to say. Like the two of you are going on a date tomorrow night."

She stared down at her feet and shrugged, but she didn't say a word.

I moved to close the space between us. "What's going on, Im? Why would you agree to go out with him?"

She shrugged, still avoiding my eye. "Why not?"

She couldn't be serious right now. We'd spent the past few weeks together, sleeping together, building something between us. I'd taken her to the shelter, a place I'd never taken any other girl because I'd didn't let many people know about that part of my life. I'd gotten to know her sister because I knew how important her family was to her. I cared about her and she had to know that, even without me saying it.

Yet here she was acting like accepting a date with another dude was no big deal.

"Why not?" I repeated, my voice harder than I meant it to be. "Because you and I are already sleeping together."

It sounded pathetic even to my ears, but I didn't know how else to say it without showing my hand. She was going on a date with another guy, I wasn't about to lay my heart at her feet only for her to trample it as she walked away from me.

She frowned up at me. "I didn't realise sneaky links came with an exclusivity clause."

My eyes widened, brows shooting up my forehead. "Did you just call me your fucking sneaky link like I'm some dirty little secret?"

"Isn't that what we are to each other? It's not like many people know about us, other than Stella and Monty."

I scoffed. "Because you wanted it that way. Not me."

She glanced away, eyes scanning the empty campus behind me like she was looking for an escape route.

Fuck me, how the hell had we ended up here? What

was going on with her? How had I read what was happening between us so wrong? Because it was becoming clear the further this conversation went on that I'd been a total idiot to think we'd been building something between us, while she was keeping me at arm's length like some token friends-with-benefits bullshit.

This was the Delaney situation all over again. I'd been falling for her while she just saw me as some casual fuck.

I was a fool for letting myself get caught up this way again.

She looked back at me, taking a deep breath and lifting her chin, those defenses of hers firmly back in place. "I don't know what to tell you. You're not my boyfriend."

I scowled. "I'm well aware I'm not your boyfriend."

"What's that supposed to mean?"

"There's no way you'd ever let me close enough for that to happen, given it would involve actually letting me in more than just your bed."

Her expression twisted with hurt, although how she thought she was the hurt one in this situation I couldn't understand.

"Screw you, Bant. Stop acting like I owe you something because you assumed what was going on between us was more than exactly what it is."

"And what was it? What are we exactly?"

Her eyes finally met mine. "Nothing more than fuck buddies."

My jaw tightened and I stared back at her. Was that really all this was to her?

She didn't wait for my response, brushing past me and hurrying down the steps. She stopped at the bottom, turning back.

"You knew what this was when it started. Don't blame me because you got attached when I warned you not to."

Fuck.

Was Marin really who she wanted? She was really choosing that idiot over me?

The thought of him touching her made me rage inside. Not because I was some competitive asshole who didn't like to lose, but because I cared about her. More than I'd let myself admit.

I blew out a long breath, running a frustrated hand through my hair. "Don't go on the date, Im."

She stared back at me, a moment of anguish crossing her face before it was gone. "You can't tell me what to do..."

I took a step towards her, closing the space between us. "Don't do it. Don't go, Imogen."

She stared down at her feet, shaking her head like she had no idea what to do. But when she looked up at me again, it was like a blow to the chest.

Resolve steeled her features and I knew I was screwed.

"I'm going on the date."

Without so much as a backwards glance, she took off down the path, hurrying away from me.

I stared after her.

How the fuck had things between us veered so far off course?

And how the hell had I ended up here again?

TWENTY-FIVE

BANT

"YO DUDE, stop playing your sad sack music. We're getting Chinese food, you in?" Jericho asked, appearing at my bedroom door.

I was lying on my bed, tossing a miniature basketball around, thinking about all the ways I'd screwed up with Imogen.

Maybe I should have called her more when I got busy? Made her come more often when we were together? Or maybe I should have just told her how I fucking felt. I'd been so concerned about her running the second I showed her any kind of real feelings, but she'd done it anyway.

Not just bolted, she'd cut and run so hard she was on a date with someone else.

I scowled. *Fucking Marin.*

I was officially pathetic for lying around on a Friday night feeling sorry for myself when the two of them were probably out having the time of their damn lives.

Sitting up, I scrubbed a hand over my face.

Fuck.

Jeri stepped further into the room, half closing the door behind him. "You all right, man?"

As teammates, we all gave each other a hard time, but I knew I could count on every single one of the jokers I lived with to be there for me when I needed them, no questions asked.

I got to my feet. "I'm good. And I'm definitely down for Chinese."

Thirty minutes later Hooker and I strolled down the main street, weighed down with bags of food. We'd ordered almost the whole damn menu.

Hooker swiped a spring roll from the bag as we walked, taking an enormous bite and moaning like he just came in his pants. "There's nothing better than Chinese food."

I quirked a brow. "Not even sex?"

He took another bite, talking around it. "Nothing is better than sex. But these spring rolls are a close second."

We passed the community center where Stella taught her art classes, rounding the corner and strolling past a bunch of restaurants, most of them packed with diners given it was prime time for dinner.

"Hey, is that Imogen?" Hooker asked, half a spring roll still hanging from his mouth as he pointed across the street.

I froze, following his gaze.

Sure enough, there was Imogen sitting at a small table in the window of the Italian place, Jackson sitting across from her. The restaurant was dimly lit, with white linen table cloths and candles on every surface. It was romantic as fuck.

"Imogen's dating Marin? I really thought she had better taste than that. That dude is a douche."

I ignored him, trying to tell myself to turn away and keep walking, but I couldn't do it. She'd straight up told me she was going to go on the date, but a small part of me had still been clinging to the hope that she'd bail on him and turn up on my doorstep instead.

Yet here she was, looking all kinds of beautiful in a pair of tight black pants and a fitted tan-colored top that clung to her perfect body in all the best ways.

She dressed up for him.

Something about that hurt more than her going on the date.

She'd taken the time to look good for him.

"Yo, Bant?" Hooker glanced at me and then back at the restaurant. "You good?"

I shook my head. Like a car crash, I couldn't tear my eyes away.

Not when Jackson and Imogen got to their feet and he helped her into her coat.

Or when she laughed at something he said as they made their way to the door.

Or when he held it open for her and she smiled at him as she stepped out.

And I definitely couldn't look away when Jackson put an arm around her waist and pulled her closer, kissing her full on the mouth.

The sight was like a twisted knife to the fucking gut.

But the worst part?

She fucking kissed him back.

TWENTY-SIX

IMOGEN

I STARTLED as Jackson's mouth landed on mine, my lips moving against his before I realized what was happening.

Hell no.

Putting a hand to his chest, I shoved him back.

His face hovered for a fraction of a second, his eyes still closed and his mouth moving as though he was still mid-kiss before he realized I was no longer there.

I had to work to keep the disdain at that sloppy excuse for a kiss from showing on my face, and resist the urge to swipe my hand over my now wet mouth.

How he thought this date had gone well enough that I'd want him to kiss me was beyond me. The thing was a fucking disaster and a total waste of make-up. Jackson had talked about himself the entire time and downed almost a whole bottle of wine while doing it. The more he drank, the worse his stories got, and I found myself glancing at the clock on the wall wondering when I could leave.

"Thanks for the hot date, I'm glad we finally got to do this." He smirked at me and I wanted to throw up.

I never should have agreed to go out with him. As far as stupid decisions went, this one was up there. Not only had I suffered through two hours of Jackson's terrible company, I'd hurt Bant in the process and I hated myself for it.

I'd screwed everything up so badly.

I was the one who told Bant to keep things between us a secret, then used it against him.

I was the one who had gotten scared and accepted a date with someone else.

I was the one who'd driven this giant wedge between us, then ended things when it wasn't what I wanted.

I was a certified head case.

I wanted to fix things with Bant, but that meant admitting to things I couldn't bring myself to. The thought of putting my heart on the line after all the pain from my past terrified me.

"So...." Jackson waggled his eyebrows at me. "Should we head back to your place?"

He had to be kidding. What part of him thought that's where this was heading? I was three seconds away from tossing my heels and bolting down the street to get away from him. Thank God I'd driven my own car instead of letting him pick me up.

"Yeah, I'm going to pass." I backed away from him, pulling my keys from my bag. "Thanks so much for dinner, the food was great."

It had been the only thing that was great about this date.

He went to protest but I just waved and turned on my heel, heading straight for my car.

I got inside, tossing my bag on the seat next to me and

grabbing my water bottle from the cup holder. I could still taste Jackson's tongue in my mouth and guilt flooded me.

I'd let him kiss me.

It had been nothing like kissing Bant. He was all soft lips and probing, panty-melting tongue.

Jackson's tongue was like sandpaper in a washing machine.

I shoved my guilt aside and started the car.

My guilt was pointless. Bant wasn't my boyfriend and going on this date tonight had been what I'd wanted.

Wasn't it?

I WAS HALFWAY to my front door when I startled at the six-foot four ball player sitting on my front step.

"Bant?" I squinted in the dark. "What are you doing here?"

Hadn't me calling him my fuck buddy been enough to drive him away? A part of me was secretly ecstatic that it hadn't, the other part was panicking that he was still here and that he might demand things of me I didn't know how to give.

He glanced up at me, those usually clear blue eyes hard. "You went on the date with him?"

My stomach dropped. "I told you I was going."

He nodded, staring off at nothing. "Yeah, you did."

He pushed to his feet, glancing down at me as he moved past me to leave. "I just never thought you'd actually do it."

Annoyance coursed through me at the way he was acting. I hated the idea that I'd hurt him, but I didn't get to this insecure place on my own. He was the one who had gone MIA the past two weeks, leaving me to spiral into insecurity about us. On top of that, my family was falling apart and he couldn't even answer my call.

Was it Bant's fault my dad had cheated or that so many guys had screwed me over in the past?

No.

But that was part of being with someone. If you committed to them, you committed to all their emotional baggage too. And I had enough to fill a damn airport.

Too many guys had screwed me over, even my own damn father when he fucked his assistant behind my mom's back, and Bant was left dealing with the fallout. Nothing about it was fair on him, but life wasn't fair.

If it was, it would have been Bant sitting across from me at that restaurant tonight. It would have been Bant pulling me closer to kiss me on the street. And it would be Bant I'd be falling asleep next to tonight.

But he was the one who had gotten too busy to call or text the past few weeks. He was the one who didn't have time to so much as hook up. And he was the one who had shown all the tell-tale signs of a guy pulling away because he didn't have the balls to end things.

He didn't get to stand in front of me now looking at me like I'd kicked his damn puppy.

"I told you the other night I was going to go, you don't get to be all butt hurt about it now."

He pivoted. "I don't get to be butt hurt? What the hell do you want me to be, Imogen? I'm into you, haven't I made that clear?"

My face twisted with outrage. "You know what you've made clear? That you're not interested. You begged me for months to spend time with you, then the moment I do suddenly you've got a crazy schedule, sending me exactly *one* text telling me we'll see each other soon. What am I supposed to think?"

I snapped my mouth shut, cringing at how needy I sounded. But at least it was the truth.

Bant ran a frustrated hand through his hair. "Fuck, is that what this whole date with Marin was about?"

I bit the inside of my cheek, fighting against the emotion clawing at my throat.

It was becoming increasingly clear I was the asshole in this situation given what I'd done tonight. He had every right to be mad at me. But I was running scared, which meant I couldn't admit to anything. To admit to my feelings would be to show my weakness and I couldn't do it. It would give him too much power over me. Power I refused to give away again to someone who would inevitably hurt me.

So instead, I was pushing him away, and I was doing it the most hurtful way possible.

I couldn't stop it though. This situation had spiralled out of control and I didn't know how to pump the brakes. I'd already admitted too much.

He stared at me like he didn't know me at all. "I knew getting into this with you that you had trust issues. But I've never given you a reason not to trust me, Imogen."

He started to walk away and a desperate, desolate kind of hurt ebbed inside of me.

I was self-sabotaging, I knew it. And in the process, I'd sabotaged us.

"I'm not the girl guys choose!" I shouted at his retreating back.

He paused, turning back to me, confusion written all over his face.

"I'm the girl they cheat on. You would have eventually done it, too."

He stalked closer, his eyes narrowed. "That's bullshit. You're the smokeshow those idiots wish they could end up with, but realize early that you're way too smart to ever fall for their shit long-term and you'll inevitably leave them. So they end it in the worst, most cowardly way before you come to your senses and kick their sorry asses to the curb." He raised his arms wide. "What can I say, most guys are insecure assholes."

"Says the guy who sleeps around and never has relationships."

I wasn't being fair and I knew it. I'd never seen him so angry, but even so, nothing he had said to me had been aggressive or unkind. He was hurt, that was plain as day. And it hurt me knowing I'd been the one to cause it. Only I couldn't undo it. I didn't know how to do that and protect myself at the same time. The only thing I could trust were my own instincts and they were screaming at me to pull back.

"I sleep around because I'm an athlete in college," Bant said, blue eyes ablaze. "It doesn't mean I don't know how to treat The One when I find her."

I crossed my arms over my chest, swallowing against the shake in my voice. "It's a shame you haven't found her then. Because smitten Bant is a sight I'd like to see."

He shook his head like he was beyond disappointed in me. "How do you know I haven't found her?"

I bit my lip at the insinuation, desperate not to let my eyes fill with the tears that wanted to come. I wouldn't break in front of him. I couldn't. I'd started this, I'd created this fissure between us. I didn't get to cry about it now.

We stood in silence and I couldn't bring myself to look him in the eye, my voice quiet.

"You would have cheated on me eventually."

He stared back at me like I'd lost it. "I would never cheat on you, Imogen."

"Yeah, well, I don't know that I believe you. It would have only been a matter of time, right?"

Hurt flashed across his face.

"You know, you might want to take a second to look at this scenario. Because if anyone could be considered the cheater in this situation, it would be you."

I forced my expression to remain neutral, ignoring his words and how right they were. Bant had always been a risk and the date with Jackson had merely been an easy way out.

I pushed my shoulders back, trying to convince myself I wasn't falling apart. "What do you want me to say? That I'm sorry?"

He stared back at me, his voice dropping low.

"Oh, I know you're not sorry for going on that date."

His jaw clenched.

"But you didn't have to fucking kiss him."

A chill spread over my entire body. How the hell did he know that? I hadn't wanted that damn kiss to happen in the first place, but the fact that Bant knew about it made my insides twist in knots.

I shook my head because it didn't matter. That kiss had served a purpose.

It was surely the final nail in whatever might have been between us.

"Well, it's a good thing we're ending it now then," I said with more confidence than I felt.

He nodded, a mix of hurt and disbelief in his eyes.

"Yeah, I guess it is."

TWENTY-SEVEN

BANT

I SAT at the kitchen counter, with my head in my hands.

What the fuck had happened last night? Not only had Imogen gone on the damn date with Marin and fucking kissed him, but when I'd called her on it, she'd ended things with me.

I'd woken up so damn angry this morning.

At myself. At her. At the situation.

I was the biggest fucking fool on campus for ending up here again after I swore I wouldn't. Only there was one major difference between this time and last — I'd come to realize I cared a hell of a lot more about Imogen than I'd ever cared about Delaney.

"Are you drunk?" Hooker asked, frowning at me like I'd grown two heads.

Davis snorted a laugh. "Hasn't touched a drop."

"So, what's he doing?"

"Pining. Wallowing. A combination of the two."

"Why?"

"Imogen."

I barely lifted my head. "Don't say her fucking name."

"Wow, dude. You've really lost it," Li said, peering at me. "What does it have to do with Imogen?"

Jericho leaned against the counter, crossing his arms over his chest. "They've been secretly hooking up for months, but she blew him off to date Jackson Marin."

Li pulled a face. "That tool on the lacrosse team? What the fuck, Imogen..."

I scrubbed my hands over my face. "Can you please stop saying her fucking name?"

The guys shared a look.

"It's pretty bad if you can't even hear her name," Hernandez piped up.

Davis spooned peanut butter from the jar straight into his mouth. "He's been in love with her for about two damn years, hence this overly dramatic reaction to it not working out."

Hooker hauled open the fridge, taking out a sports drink and popping the cap. "Now I get why you were like a statue on the sidewalk when we saw them at the restaurant last night."

Davis' brows crept up his forehead and I shook my head. *Don't ask.*

Hooker poured out the sports drink into five red cups, then pulled a bottle of vodka from the freezer. He added the spirit to each, then handed them out, adding an extra splash to mine before sliding it in front of me.

"Makes sense you look like someone robbed your grandma given you just lost the girl you've been pining over for years."

I scowled. "I haven't been fucking pining."

Davis chuckled. "Dude, you've been pining. You just covered it by insulting her a lot like you were in the third grade."

Ignoring my teammates, I knocked back the entire drink in one go, relishing the vodka burn in my throat. My phone buzzed on the counter beside me, an incoming call from Van.

"I've got to take this," I said, sliding from my seat and heading into the hall. "Hey."

"Stella called and said you and Imogen had broken up and you might be in need of a friend."

I sighed, preparing for the inevitable grilling.

"Imagine my surprise at learning you and Imogen were dating in the first place. You didn't think I'd want to know that interesting piece of information when we spoke last week?"

"To be honest, I thought Stella would tell you the night she caught me sneaking into their place at one am."

Van laughed down the phone. "Classic Bant. And my girl is loyal, she knows how to keep a secret."

"She keep all of yours for you?"

"Please, I don't have any secrets, I'm an open book."

Silence passed for a beat.

"I'm sorry, bro," Van said.

I leaned against the wall. "It's fine. It's... whatever."

"Right, sure it is."

He paused and I knew him well enough to know what was coming.

"You're in love with her, aren't you?"

I stared down at my shoes, the phone pressed to my ear. "I don't know, man..."

There was no mistaking the smile in my best friend's voice. "Yeah, you do."

I shoved a hand through my hair. "Fine. I'm in love with her, but there's no fucking point in me admitting that, other than for your own twisted amusement. She doesn't feel the same way and she made that pretty damn clear when she ended things and went on a date with someone else."

There was shuffling from the other end of the phone.

"What are you doing?"

"I'm booting up my computer. I'm booking you a ticket to New York next weekend. We don't have a game, I was meant to go upstate with some teammates to unwind, but I'm blowing it off. Get your ass to the city and get drunk with me. You can go see your mom. A weekend away will fix everything."

I huffed a laugh. "Did it fix everything for you and Stella when you went to party with your brother in Houston?"

He practically growled in response. His relationship with Stella had gone to shit after that trip. He'd come back and broken up with her over a misunderstanding with his brother and had broken Stella's heart in the process. The idiot was lucky she'd forgiven him.

"Do you want your free trip or not?"

"Yes, I do. Please, Daddy Warbucks, let me come spend the weekend with you in the big city."

There was a smile in his voice. "I'm emailing you the ticket now. Pack your bags."

THE SECOND I stepped off the plane, Van took me to a bar in midtown. We were parked in a booth, ordering whiskey on the rocks in an endless stream of liquor.

"So, you finally wore Imogen down, huh?" Van said, toying with his glass. "Only took you a couple of years."

"You had to bring her up just when I'm starting to enjoy myself?"

He smirked. "You've been panting after her for so long, but I never thought she'd cave."

I levelled him with a look. "Gee, thanks a lot, bro. Since when has there been a babe I can't charm?"

"Please, there have been plenty. Clearly your ego has run away with you since West and I left. I might need to word up Davis about keeping you in better check."

"Don't worry about it. Imogen ditching me for that asshole Marin has shredded my ego."

He stared at me, eyes assessing.

"Imogen is the first girl you've liked since Delaney..."

The words hung between us and I wanted to pretend like they'd never been said. I stared at my drink, tilting the amber liquid along the side of the glass.

"I liked her more than I ever liked Del."

Van's eyes widened. "Well, shit..."

I shifted in my seat. "Yeah."

"At least it wasn't your teammate this time?"

My eyes narrowed on him and I resisted the urge to junk punch him under the table.

"Still too soon to joke about it?" Van chuckled.

"I don't know if I'll ever be able to joke about a girl I thought I was in love with hooking up with my teammate."

"Thought you were in love with? I'd say back then you were pretty damn sure of it."

I gave him a rueful smile. "That was before."

"Before Imogen?"

A heavy silence descended, all the words I wasn't saying

hanging between us. But Van was my best friend so he understood them anyway.

I was about to pipe up and swiftly change the subject, when a tall figure loomed over the table.

"What a cute little reunion this is," West said, smirking down at us. "Did you forget to invite me?"

We both got to our feet in surprise, slapping him on the back in a man-hug.

"What the hell are you doing here?" I asked, sliding back into the booth.

Van shifted over so West could slide in beside him. "How long are you here, is the better question."

"You've got me for four hours, then I need to be on a plane back to Washington."

I raised my brows. "They've got you on a short leash."

West chuckled. "They can have me on any leash they want, so long as I get to keep hitting the court every game and they keep paying me to do it."

"You like being restrained? Kinky. Monty is a lucky lady."

West shook his head at me, flagging down the waitress and ordering a drink.

A minute later a whiskey appeared in front of him and he took a sip, turning serious. "So, what have I missed?"

I sighed. "Just the fucking dumpster fire that is my life."

Van lifted his glass. "Bant just admitted he likes Imogen more than he ever liked Delaney."

West's eyes widened in surprise. "No fucking way."

I nodded sourly. Not that any of it mattered now.

Van shifted forward, forearms on the table. "You know Imogen likes you, right?"

I huffed a laugh. "Yeah, she made that real clear when she kissed Marin."

"She's scared of commitment, Bant. Same as you. I'm not trying to make excuses for her, but I can kind of understand why she did what she did."

I scowled, surprised he was defending her when he was supposed to be my best friend.

"What Delaney did to you was fucked up," West said. "You were so into her and she massively messed with your head. But put yourself in Imogen's position... from what Monty says, she's dated a lot of assholes and been Delaney'd more than once." He shrugged. "I can understand her being afraid to put herself on the line again."

I stared at my glass, mulling it over.

"You both have crap from your past interfering with your present," Van added. "But maybe if you'd told Imogen how you felt, things would have worked out differently."

Annoyance flared inside me and I couldn't tell if it was directed at myself or Imogen.

So, she had trust issues. Didn't we all? Delaney sleeping with Tanner behind my back had massively fucked with my head. I'd sworn off relationships and committed myself to casual hook-ups. What Delaney did changed me for the worse. But with Imogen, I'd wanted to be different, because she was different. In her, I'd found everything I never knew I wanted.

Yet for her... I hadn't been worth it to put her issues aside and try. She chose to cling to those insecurities and use them to drive a wedge between us.

I hadn't been enough for Delaney. And now I wasn't enough for Imogen either.

The thought shredded me.

And I couldn't get the image of her kissing Jackson out of my fucking head.

Whatever I'd hoped might have been between Imogen

and I was done, she'd made damn sure of it. I was an idiot if I spent one more second moping over a girl who'd told me I was nothing but a good time for her and went and locked lips with another guy.

It was useless pining for the kind of relationship Van had with Stella or West had with Monty. It just wasn't in the cards for me. I'd tried it twice now and both times it had come back to bite me in the ass.

"I know you. The casual hook ups were fun for a while, but deep down that's not what you want," Van said.

Knocking back the rest of my drink, I looked my best friends in the eye.

"That's too bad, because I'm officially done trying for more."

I smiled gratefully at the waitress as she placed another round on the table in front of me.

"Getting your heart pummelled will do that to you."

TWENTY-EIGHT

IMOGEN

"ARE you currently involved in some intense mating ritual with the couch that I don't know about? You haven't gotten off that thing in days."

Stella strode into the living room, dropping her book bag by the door.

I forced myself into a sitting position to make room for her.

"Bant and I are done."

Her eyes widened with surprise as she dropped down onto the cushion. "Did he break up with you? Because I'm not above kicking his ass."

I shook my head. "I ended it."

"Why? What happened?"

Tears pricked the backs of my eyes and I tried to fight them, clutching my blanket to my chest. "I screwed up, Stell."

She scooted closer, giving my knee a squeeze.

"He found out about the date with Jackson and called me out for it. I was hurt because he'd been ignoring me and I convinced myself that he was pulling away. Not to mention, I was all emotional about the stuff with my parents, and instead of just admitting I was being an asshole and trying to push him away, I broke it off with him."

She winced. "I can understand him being upset, but you and Bant weren't exclusive. You're allowed to date other people."

I lost the emotional battle with myself, tears sliding down my cheeks. "I shouldn't have done it. I was falling for him and I got scared and hurt him."

Before Stella could respond, the front door opened and Monty breezed through.

"Honey, I'm home!" she sing-songed. She strolled into the living room, took one look at my face and her expression fell. "What's happened? Who do I need to murder?"

I shook my head. "You can't murder Bant."

"The hell I can't. What did he do?"

"They broke up," Stella offered. "Imogen went on the date with Jackson and ended things with Bant."

Monty's eyes widened. "You're dating Jackson now?"

"No!"

She perched on the armrest behind me. "Oh, thank God, because there was no way I was going to be able to pretend to like that guy."

I sniffled a laugh. "The date was a disaster. I was a coward to ever accept it. But the worst part is, he kissed me and somehow Bant found out."

Monty pulled a face. "He saw the two of you. I overheard him telling Jeri. I love you, but kissing Jackson when you're this into Bant probably wasn't your best move."

"I didn't kiss him! He jumped me on the street after spending the entire night mainlining red wine and exhausting me with boring stories about himself." I dropped my face in my hands. "I've made such a fucking mess of everything. I'm an idiot."

Stella brushed my hair back from my face, tucking it behind my ear. "Yeah, but a loveable idiot."

I laughed, raising my head. "You can't call me an idiot when I'm crying."

"Really? Because I definitely did and you've survived it."

Monty turned serious. "Hey Im, can I ask you something?"

I nodded, wiping my nose with the back of my hand with all the grace of a bridge troll.

"Did Bant ever tell you about Delaney?"

"No, but we bumped into her on campus a few weeks ago. He got all weird and closed off. I assumed she was some crazy ex who was still into him."

Stella shook her head. "Delaney and Bant dated when they were both freshmen. Apparently, he was really into her, like, more than he has ever been into any girl."

"So, what happened?"

"Bant found her in bed with his teammate and best friend at the time."

I stilled.

"It was bad, Im. The other guy, Tanner, not only dropped out of the team, he eventually dropped out of Pierson. West said that before it all went down, Bant had been talking about ring shopping for Delaney."

Bant? Ring shopping? As a freshman?

Anger seared through me. Delaney had betrayed him with his best friend.

...But had I been any better?

Bant and I had been building something, a connection forming between us, and I'd betrayed him just as she had. Granted it hadn't been with his best friend but the feelings would have been exactly the same.

Guilt and regret flooded me so hard my chest ached.

"She's the reason Bant is the way he is," Monty said, stroking my hair. "After she broke his heart, he swore off all women and refused to get close to anyone. Until you."

While I'd thought I was saving myself from a playboy who would inevitably hurt me, I'd ended up hurting Bant in the worst possible way by inadvertently using his biggest fear against him.

I dropped my face in my hands. "What have I done?"

Monty and Stella shifted closer, wrapping their arms around me.

"You couldn't know something he wouldn't tell you. And you didn't mean to hurt him, you did what you thought was best for you," Stella said, rubbing my back. "It'll be okay, Imogen, I promise."

I lifted my head. "How can you possibly know that?"

"Because we've seen the way he looks at you," Monty said. "He's going to forgive you."

Right now, I didn't think I deserved to be forgiven.

TURNS out I was both an asshole *and* a coward.

Despite knowing I'd hurt Bant in the worst possible way and knowing the right course of action would be to go to him and apologize, I did neither.

Instead, I avoided him.

I made excuses not to go to the basketball house whenever Monty or one of the guys invited me there, claimed I had assignments due whenever I was expected to go to a basketball game, and I'd even ducked behind a tree when I'd seen Bant walking across campus with Li and Davis.

I was officially pathetic and it was all my own doing.

I'd screwed up and I was too proud to admit it and make it right.

Just seeing him on campus had made my chest ache. I missed him so much. I missed the feel of his body next to mine, his arm around my shoulders, and his cocky, self-assured comebacks to just about everything I said. I even missed that infuriating smirk.

But still my pride wouldn't let me go to him and fix what I'd broken.

Just how damaged was I? I'd promised myself I wouldn't let another guy affect me the way the ones from my past had. Yet, I was still letting them ruin my life. I wasn't equipped to study psychology, I needed a psychological assessment instead.

The tipping point came Friday night when I was sitting at home alone while almost everyone I knew was at a party at the basketball house. Monty had tried to convince me to come. She'd made me promise to, in fact. Only I'd bailed at the last minute.

Wandering into the kitchen at home, bored out of my mind, I imagined just how much fun Stella and Monty were having right now without me.

I slid a slice of last night's pizza from the fridge and took a bite. Leaning against the counter, I dialed Monty's number.

Music blared in the background the moment she picked up.

"Im," she shouted over the noise. "Imogen, where are

you? Why aren't you here?"

"I couldn't do it. I didn't want to face him."

She knew exactly which *him* I was referring to.

Monty murmured something, the phone rustling, then a door closed on her end and the sound of the party faded.

"Is he there?" I asked, hoping he was at the library or Ruby's. Anywhere else.

"He lives here... so yeah, he's here."

"What's he doing?"

Monty paused and it made my chest tightened.

"You can tell me," I pressed, squeezing my eyes shut. It was like a car accident I couldn't look away from. I didn't want to know but at the same time, I needed to.

"He's pretty wasted and pretty cut up about what went down between you two, but trying to pretend he's not. Typical Bant, really."

I bit my lip. It was eating away at me too. Yet, I still couldn't bring myself to fix it. Fixing it meant laying my heart on the line and the thought made me want to throw up.

"He's..." Monty stopped.

"I'm a big girl, you can tell me."

"He's not alone, Im. Some girl is all over him."

My heart sank to my shoes and I dropped my head, phone still pressed to my ear. "Well, I guess that's it then."

"No, that's not it. He's crazy about you. West said he's never seen him like this over a girl before. He claims it's worse than with Delaney."

I snorted. "Is that why he's currently wrapped around someone else?"

"He's hurt, Im. You can see it. He's drunk and acting stupid." Monty sighed. "Can you please just come here? Come and maybe work it out?"

I shook my head even though she couldn't see it. Going there and watching Bant make out with some jersey chasing hottie was the last thing I wanted to do.

"I think I'll sit this one out. Bant is a big boy, he's exactly where he wants to be right now."

Monty's voice softened. "What about you? Are you exactly where you want to be?"

———

WITH MONTY'S words still ringing in my ears, I strolled up the path to the basketball house, the thumping bass of the music loud enough to wake the whole street.

I kinda wanted to throw up.

I'd sat on the couch at home wallowing in self-pity for all of fifteen minutes before throwing open my closet and pulling out my most killer black dress and heels. The dress hugged my curves in all the right places, my chest practically spilling out the front while somehow still managing to look classy.

Turning up here was probably a monumentally stupid idea, but I was good at being stupid lately. Great at it, in fact.

The moment I pushed through the front door I was met with a wall of heat from all the bodies in the house. Smiling at people I knew from my classes or yoga, I made my way through the crowd, stopping short at the doorway to the living room.

I'd thought after hearing Monty say it, it wouldn't hurt seeing Bant with a girl draped in his lap.

I was wrong.

So very, very wrong.

Hurt I had absolutely no right to feel burned through me at the way she clung to him. His hand was around her waist like she belonged there. He leaned forward, glassy-eyed as he spoke to Hooker. The girl shifted in his lap, trying to regain his attention, and he glanced her way, whispering something in her ear.

My chest caved and I turned away, threading my way through the party to the kitchen.

I'd pushed him away and now he was gone. I didn't get to feel any kind of way about it.

Monty was leaning against the counter in the kitchen, laughing with Davis.

"Imogen!" She rushed me, pulling me into a hug. "Holy shit, you look amazing! Bant is going to lose his mind when he sees you."

I smiled ruefully. "Evidently not. I saw him in the living room with a girl attached to him."

Davis shook his head. "He's pretty fucked up over everything. He probably wouldn't notice his own reflection right now and we know how much Bant loves a mirror."

Monty snorted a laugh. "Rich coming from you, D."

Li appeared, dishing out drinks. "You look like you could use a shot, Im."

He passed one to me and I peered into the cup. "What is it?"

"Does it matter?"

I tilted my head at him. Good point. I didn't wait for my friends, knocking back the shot in one gulp and discarding the cup on the counter.

A young guy with dark hair and killer green eyes

dressed in a Pierson Basketball t-shirt sidled up to the group.

"Who's your friend, Davis?" he asked, eyes on me.

I glanced at Monty in question and she rolled her eyes. The guy had to be a freshman from his youthful face and the way he was openly staring. But after the week I'd had, wallowing in my own hurt and undoing, I was all too willing to let a freshman tell me I was pretty.

I turned to him, one hand on my hip. "If you want to know my name, how about you ask me?"

A slow smile spread across his pretty face. "I'm Culley, what's your name?"

I tilted my head to the side, my eyes running over him the same way his had over me.

"Imogen."

I offered him my hand. He took it, giving it a small shake then using it to subtly close the space between us. I didn't miss the amused glance Li and Davis shared, like Culley was a constant source of entertainment. The guy was smooth and definitely not lacking in confidence.

"You look like you're in need of a drink, Imogen," Culley offered.

"I am pretty thirsty."

He towed me to the cooler on the counter. "Let's fix that."

Monty threw a glance edged with concern my way, which I ignored, downing another two rounds of shots. I'd need alcohol if I was going to get through tonight.

Two drinks later, Culley was leading me into the living room to the makeshift dance floor. The music was loudest in there, a small group of writhing bodies gathered in the dark room in front of the empty fireplace.

Culley's arms came around my waist and he leaned in, his lips brushing my shoulder. "You're so fucking hot."

I swayed my hips against him, pretending he was someone else. Someone who might even be in this room right now, but the throng of bodies meant I couldn't see him.

We danced for two songs before a sexy RnB number came on and I turned in Culley's arms, his hands sliding over my waist to pull me tighter against him. He was hot and attentive and I pushed away the feeling that I was somehow betraying Bant all over again.

But we weren't even on speaking terms. He was wrapped up in some other girl right now, whatever had been between us was long over. I'd killed it stone dead when I'd gone on that date with Jackson.

Regret coursed through me and I pulled away from Culley, putting the smallest bit of space between our bodies.

The crowd parted, giving me a glimpse of Bant in the armchair, the blonde still perched in his lap. He did a lazy sweep of the room. His eyes landed on mine and he froze, his expression darkening.

I held my breath, waiting for his reaction.

I expected him to turn away and pretend I didn't exist, and I knew it was going to tear me open when he did. If he dismissed me, it meant he truly didn't care anymore.

Instead, his eyes never left me as he lifted the blonde from his lap, ignoring her protests as he got to his feet and made his way roughly through the crowded room.

His blue eyes were dark with anger. "What the hell is this?"

Culley glanced up at him, confused and probably a

little drunk. "Dancing, dude." Then he leaned down and pressed his lips just below my ear, making me cringe.

Bant shoved his teammate in the shoulder. "All right, beat it, Culley."

He stumbled back a step, his face pinching in annoyance. "What the hell, dude...?"

"You're done here," Bant said, cutting him off.

Culley glanced at me, then back at Bant, who was practically vibrating with fury. Then he shrugged and backed away, disappearing into the crowd.

Bant turned back to me. "Dating Marin wasn't enough, now you want my teammate too?"

I faltered, the blood draining from my face. I hadn't thought this through. While I'd clocked the basketball t-shirt Culley had been wearing, I'd never registered that dancing with him would be make me Delaney all over again.

"Bant, it isn't like that..."

His gaze roamed over me, those bright blue eyes usually filled with humor now hard-edged. He clenched his jaw, a muscle in his cheek twitching.

I waited for him to say something or to curse at me or to storm off.

To my utter surprise, he moved closer, his hand sliding over my hip and curving around my waist to tug me to him. Our bodies pressed together and my eyes widened in surprise. Having his arms around me again was everything I'd wanted. And so much more than I deserved, given the way I'd hurt him.

My hands landed on his shoulders to steady me. He didn't utter a word as our bodies moved together to the music.

He smelled like he'd been bathing in whiskey, but I

didn't care. I wanted to slide my hands around his neck. I wanted to press my lips to the base of his throat. I wanted to tug him to the laundry room and go at it like we had at movie night. But I was afraid if I so much as flinched too hard, he'd pull away, and I was desperate to keep him.

His lips brushed over my hair and he breathed me in. He took another breath like he was about to say something, then thought better of it, silence hanging between us.

The party raged around us but all I could focus on was him and the way he felt against me.

Steeling myself, I slid my hands around his neck, threading my fingers through his hair. His head dropped to my shoulder, his lips caressing my skin in the briefest kiss.

If I wanted to fix things between us, I needed to say something. To tell him how I felt.

I swallowed, afraid of the words I was about to utter.

"I've missed you."

His whole body went rigid in my arms and my heart pounded in my chest. He didn't say anything.

"Bant, did you hear me?"

His face was still at my shoulder but I didn't miss the hard way he said "I heard you."

I was about to repeat my words, when his hands dropped from my body and he pulled back. "I can't do this."

His expression was twisted with a mix of anger and anguish. He turned and pushed through the crowd without another word.

I stared after him, embarrassed at being left in the middle of a dance floor.

But, what did I have to lose at this point? I'd already lost everything that meant anything to me.

I pushed through the crowd after him, spotting him as

he made his way up the stairs. I followed, bursting into his room to find him pacing by the window.

"What do you want, Imogen? What else could you possibly want from me?"

He ran a frustrated hand through his hair, his toned biceps flexing.

God, he's so damn hot. Why didn't I appreciate it when I had the chance?

"To talk to you."

He scowled. "I have nothing to say."

I stepped further into the room, closing the distance between us.

"Bant, come on, just talk to me."

He stopped pacing, staring out the window, the muscles of his toned back contracting with tension.

"I'm sorry for everything with Jackson—" I started, but he ignored me, moving past me and heading for the door.

He shook his head. "I meant it when I said I can't do this."

"Bant, please..."

My fingers closed around his arm, the contact lighting some kind of fire inside him and he rounded on me. "I said I can't do this right now."

I went to move closer but he stepped away, as though it physically pained him to be close to me. Did he really hate me that much, that even being in the same space as me was an effort? It wasn't that long ago that he'd claimed being close to me was his favorite place to be. Couldn't we get back there?

I shook my head, confused. "Why can't you just talk to me?"

He ran two frustrated hands through his hair. "Because you broke my fucking heart, Imogen! Don't you get that?"

I faltered, stumbling back a step.

"You made it clear whatever was between us was just fucking around for you. But I'm fucking in love with you, and watching you kiss that idiot Marin shredded me."

My heart pounded in my chest, the shots I'd done with Culley churning in my stomach.

"I... I'm sorry."

He shook his head. "No, you're not. And I don't care anymore. We've both been drinking, now isn't the time to talk about this or we're both going to say things we regret."

Was that him telling me that he already regretted telling me he loved me?

I'd already hurt him deeper than I'd ever known, and I didn't want to push things with him any more than I already had.

I headed for the door, hovering in the doorway for a moment, the words he'd just uttered tearing me open inside.

"If it makes you feel any better, I broke my own heart too."

MONTY AND STELLA found me face down on Monty's bed an hour later.

"Shit, Imogen, what happened?"

"If Bant was an asshole to you, I'll kick his ass down the stairs," Stella said, the threat lacking punch coming from her pacifist mouth. The girl wouldn't so much as kill a spider.

I murmured into the pillow, refusing to sit up and face what I'd done.

"Sorry, what was that?" Stella said, brushing my hair back from my shoulder.

I rolled over, my face stained with tears. I'd never cried as much in my life as I had the past week.

"I broke his fucking heart."

Monty's eyes widened. "Did he tell you that?"

I nodded, and Stella and Monty shared a look.

"Okay," Stella said, flopping down on the bed beside me and clapping her hands. "Pull yourself together because I have a plan that is *guaranteed* to fix this."

TWENTY-NINE

IMOGEN

I COULD HEAR the roar of the crowd before I'd even set foot in the stadium. Pausing at the door, I adjusted the Pierson basketball jersey hugging my torso.

After Monty, Stella and I had locked ourselves away in Monty's room at the party, my two best friends had helped me come up with a plan to win back the guy I'd hurt more than I was willing to admit.

I strode into the stadium now, forcing my head high.

The damn plan better work or I was going to look like a desperate groupie who couldn't comprehend when something was over.

Squeaking shoes and the pounding of the ball echoed across the court as I scanned the stands, spotting Stella and Monty three rows back.

"You look so freaking hot, he's going to love it," Stella said, squeezing my hand.

"This better work."

"It will, don't worry," Monty said, leaning around Stella.

There was only seven minutes left in the game before the players would head to the locker room. It would be at least another fifteen before they started to emerge, which meant in about twenty-five minutes I would be laying my heart at Bant's feet and praying he wasn't going to stomp all over it.

My palms were sweating and there was a knot in my stomach the size of a semi-truck.

"Here," Monty said, handing me a cup of beer. "Drink this, you'll feel better."

I took the cup, the idea of filling my stomach with alcohol making it churn, but I sipped at it anyway hoping it would calm my nerves.

The final buzzer sounded and the crowd went crazy. Pierson won by seven points.

My heart pounded in my chest at the sight of Bant laughing with his teammates as they celebrated. Not so long ago, he'd been smiling at me that way. Then I'd gone and ruined everything because I was too insecure to trust in what I wanted. Or him and what we'd had.

"It's going to work out, Im. I know it." Stella gave me an encouraging smile, she and Monty sidling past me.

"You've got this," Monty added. "We'll see you back at the house."

I nodded, taking a seat to wait for Bant to emerge from the locker room. What felt like a lifetime later, players started to slowly trickle out, people waiting to greet them. Bant was one of the last through the doors, walking out with Davis, who smirked as I approached.

"Got my name on your back tonight, Im?"

I gave him a tight smile. "Uh, no actually..."

I chanced a look at Bant, his expression completely shuttered, no trace of what he might be feeling at seeing me.

Davis motioned for me to turn, letting out a low whistle when I did, both of them reading the name on my jersey.

Bantempelli.

"Glad you realized the way to his heart is through his ego," Davis said, grinning.

Bant's gaze slid to his teammate. "Don't you have somewhere else you need to be? Like inside a cheerleader's skirt?"

"You know, I really don't. Thought I might stick around for this entertainment." Davis motioned between the two of us, but one hard look from Bant had him rethinking it and he sauntered off.

"What are you doing here?" Bant asked, not unkindly, but not exactly friendly either.

"I need to talk to you." I twisted my fingers together, attempting a joke to ease the awkward tension between us. "Figured I'd wait out here this time and not try to talk to you in the showers."

I'd been hoping for at least a hint of a smile at the shared memory, but he gave me nothing, his expression stony.

"I'm listening."

His whole closed demeanour was throwing me off and sending my nerves ratcheting towards the sky. I'd thought the jersey might go some way towards softening him. Now that I was standing in front of him and he was looking at me like I'd never mattered to him at all, my confidence faltered.

I pushed aside the negative voice in my head. Whatever happened, he deserved to know the truth about how I felt about him. I owed him that much.

"I'm sorry for going on the date with Jackson. I was

stupid and scared and selfish and I'm sorry I did it. I promise you, I never meant to kiss him. I didn't want it."

I bit the inside of my cheek, waiting for him to respond. Those hard blues stared back at me.

I wanted him to smile at me like he had at his teammates at the end of the game. I wanted him to reach out and pull me in like he had at the party or throw an arm around my shoulders and tuck me at his side like we'd strolled through campus so many times. I wanted his mouth to drop to mine and his hands on my ass.

I wanted to be close to him again.

Instead, he was looking at me like I was a stranger.

I'd given up the right to want those things, to expect them from him, the moment I'd accepted that date with Jackson.

And again when I'd told him he was nothing but my fuck buddy.

And again when I'd said it was over.

"Thanks for the apology." He shifted on his feet, glancing around the stadium. "Is that all?"

I bit my lip to stem the tears pricking the backs of my eyes. I'd hurt him so badly and I didn't know how to fix it. The only way was to lay my heart on the line and hope for the best, because the worst was already here.

He went to walk away but I reached out, grabbing his arm. He stared down at the contact, then back at me.

"I want you to know that I'm falling for you."

The twitch of his brow was the only reaction he gave.

"I have been for a while and I didn't know what to do with it. But I am. I'm falling for you."

I searched his face for even the smallest hint of reciprocation. What I was offering him was more than I'd ever offered any guy. I was standing out on a shaking limb and praying he'd reach out and pull me in.

"That's it?"

My heart stuttered at his words, my stomach sinking.

"That's the best you have to offer? You're falling for me?"

His tone wasn't harsh, but it wasn't soft either. It was totally and utterly inscrutable.

"Bant, please..." I rubbed at my chest, trying to stem the sudden ache there at the way he was looking at me. "I don't know what else you want me to say."

I'd opened my heart to him, something he knew didn't come easily for me, and this was his response? To claim it wasn't good enough and demand more?

He moved closer, eyes blazing. "I want you to say that there's no one else in the world for you but me and you finally see it. I want you to tell me that all the bickering and fighting and the bullshit between us was just covering the inconvenient truth we were both trying so hard to ignore."

He ducked his head so we were eye to eye and it was suddenly hard to breathe.

"I want you to tell me that you love me, the same way I love you. That I'm all you can think about. That you've been fucking miserable these past few weeks and that I'm all you want from this point on."

He waited, eyes bouncing between mine. Seconds passed but the words didn't come.

Another beat passed and his expression shuttered.

He pulled back, nodding.

"You know... I knew going into this with you that getting you to open up to me would be hard. Or damn near impossible. But I at least thought you'd have something to say about it when I tell you I love you. That's twice now and... nothing." He spread his arms wide in defeat, slowly backing away. "Have a nice life, Im. You deserve it."

He dropped his arms and turned on his heel, shoving his hands in the pockets of his jacket and striding away from me.

Something shattered in my chest at the knowledge that this was it. I was going to lose him.

I'd fucked this up so badly. Even trying to fix it, I'd royally screwed it up.

But I wanted to be better.

I had to try again. And again and again and again, if that's what it took to win him back.

"Wait!" I called after him, but he didn't stop, just kept striding away from me like he didn't even hear me. I ran after him. "Bant, please wait!"

He halted, turning to face me. "What am I waiting for? You still don't know what you want and I'm not going to wait around for you to work it out. Go date other guys, see if you can find anything even close to what we have. I know that you won't, but clearly you still need to work it out."

I stepped in front of him, my chest heaving. I was terrified, but even mad at me he was telling me exactly how he felt. He deserved to hear it in return.

"You're all I can think about," I blurted, my hands shaking. "I've been fucking miserable these past few weeks."

A ghost of a smile played at the corners of his mouth as I repeated the words he'd demanded from me back to him.

"You're all I want from this point on because I love you, the same way you love me."

He stared back at me in the longest moment of my life.

I trembled all over, swallowing against the lump that had formed in my throat at putting myself out there and exposing myself so deeply. I prayed he wouldn't walk away from me again, because I had nothing else to offer him. It really would be the end.

Those blue eyes studied me, revealing nothing of what was going on inside his head.

Then his face split in that signature grin that made my heart skip a beat. "Are you just telling me what I want to hear?"

Relief overwhelmed me in a rush. He'd made a joke.

I gave him a watery smile, trying not to cry. "Bant, I swear, if you make me jump through any more hoops..."

He softened, his hand reaching out to close around my waist and pull me closer.

"Alright, alright, you love me, no need to cry about it." He grinned down at me.

I tried and failed to cling to the annoyance that usually flared inside me when he acted this way, but I was just so grateful he was touching me.

Then his mouth dropped to mine, his breath warm against my lips.

"I love you, too. I think I've been sort of in love with you from the first night we met when you told me nobody says lady killer anymore and asked me if my sleazy brand of charm worked on women."

I smiled at the memory and his fingers tangled in my hair, our bodies pressing together. "FYI, it doesn't."

He squeezed my waist. "Oh yeah? Seems like it's worked pretty well on you given you just told me you're in love with me."

I shrugged a 'maybe' in response. "You've really loved me that long?"

"Yeah, Im. I've loved you that long. I just never thought I'd have a chance in hell of you feeling the same way."

I stared at him in disbelief. All the losers I'd wasted time with, the cheaters I'd unwittingly let use me, and Luke Bantempelli had been there nearly the whole time with a killer smile, insane body and a witty cutback.

"Gotta say... you lost for words is hot." His eyes lit with amusement and I smacked at his shoulder.

"Mock me some more and see how far it gets you."

His arms wrapped around my waist, his giant body enveloping me. "Fuck, I love it when you're mad."

I rolled my eyes. "Shut up and kiss me."

EPILOGUE

IMOGEN

"HERE'S TO FUCKING GRADUATING!" Hernandez shouted as we knocked our glasses together.

I glanced around O'Reilly's, everyone I cared about at Pierson in one room.

Jericho, Hernandez, Davis, Bant, Monty, Stella, and I were all still in our gowns from graduation, all of us hugging our families and heading straight for the bar to settle in for a long night of celebrating.

My parents had both shown up for my graduation and sat on opposite sides of the event. Naomi, ever the peacemaker, had sat with my dad, while Lola had sided with Mom. Mom had refused to so much as look at my dad when they'd both congratulated me after the ceremony. I guess this was my life now, but I didn't blame Mom for wanting nothing to do with him. I still had no idea how I felt about him.

West and Van had gotten a leave pass from their teams to see Monty and Stella get their diplomas, although both had so far spent more time being accosted by fans wanting pictures with them. Stella was taking it in her stride, while Monty was getting more and more agitated by the second at having West's attention stolen away, something he found endlessly amusing and hadn't stopped ribbing her about.

Bant pushed to his feet, reaching out to kiss me on the head. "I'm getting another round," he declared to the table, pushing through the crowd towards the bar.

"I can't believe we actually made it to graduation," Stella said, looking a little bummed that it was all over.

"Some of us almost didn't," Monty piped up and West's arm tightened around her neck, pulling her closer.

He whispered something in her ear and she smiled up at him, the two of them sharing a quick kiss.

We'd all be going our separate ways soon and I was going to miss every single one of them. Our time at Pierson had been a rollercoaster, but I knew I was going to look back on the four years I'd spent here and realize they were some of the best of my life. Every single person at the table held a special place in my heart. Even Hooker.

Starting to sweat in my gown, I downed my drink and reached for the clasp at my neck, ditching it and hanging it over the back of the booth.

"Jeeeeeeeesus, Imogen." Davis whistled, his eyes roaming over the tight leather pants and fitted corset top I'd been sporting under my gown. "That outfit has me willing to risk Bant's fist to my face just for a shot with you."

I laughed, Bant returning from the bar with a tray of drinks. He took one look at me and tossed the tray on the table, spilling half of them. He crowded me in an instant, backing me into the wall, his hands pawing at my waist and ass.

I grinned up at him. "You okay there, big guy?"

He shook his head. "Who the hell gave you permission to take my fucking breath away with this outfit?"

"Aw, that's so sweet."

"And make my dick uncomfortably hard behind my zipper."

I sighed. "There's the playboy I know so well. Sweet really doesn't suit you anyway."

He scowled. "Please, I'll show you how sweet I can be."

I quirked a brow. "Oh yeah?"

His mouth dropped to my throat, his warm lips brushing the sensitive skin and making me shiver. He pushed his body against mine, shielding us from view as his hand roamed over my breasts.

"Bant, we're in a packed bar," I said, my voice breathless.

His mouth moved to the sensitive spot behind my ear, making me melt. He kissed along my jaw, stopping at my lips. "I don't care, I fucking want you."

"You had me three times last night."

He pulled back, staring down at me. "No matter how many times I have you, it'll never be enough. You're my whole fucking world, Imogen. You know that right?"

I bit my lip and nodded, wishing like hell we weren't in a public place right now because I wanted to climb him like a tree.

We'd wasted so much time hating each other.

"Would you two cut it out already?" Monty called across the room. "I'm the one with a boyfriend who lives in another state and you don't see us mauling each other in public."

I gently pushed at Bant's chest and he stepped back, taking my hand and towing me back to the table. He pulled up a chair at the side of the booth and took a seat, tugging me onto his lap. Whenever we were together, he had to be touching me at all times.

"Are you two ever going to explain your drunken tattoos?" Stella reached for the pitcher of beer in the middle of the table. Van took it from her, pouring it out, then slung an arm around her shoulders. She leaned into him and I didn't miss the look of pure adoration he'd always had for her when he stared down at her.

He was going to propose any day now. I could feel it.

"Who cares?" Hooker asked. "They're embarrassing. Bant's is a damn curved line and Imogen's is two dots. You sure you weren't high at the time and not drunk?"

Jericho laughed. "Don't be bitter because you have fomo, Hooker. One day you'll find a girl willing to tattoo herself for you."

Hooker scoffed but didn't deny it.

"If you want to see it so badly..." I offered.

Our friends all turned to us and I held out a hand, Bant doing the same. Our palms brushed over each other, our index fingers aligning. When the curved half circle of Bant's tattoo met the two dots of mine it created a perfect smiley face.

"You've got to be fucking kidding me," Davis said, bursting into laughter.

"That's the amazing tattoo you geniuses decided on? Remind me never to invite you to my parties," Hernandez said, shaking his head.

A smile spread across my face as I glanced down at Bant. He reached up, his fingers tangling in my hair and he tugged me closer, lips brushing mine.

"There's no one I'd rather get drunk with, listen to smutty audiobooks with, or get stupid tattoos with."

My smile widened. "That's good to know, playboy." I pressed my mouth to his, both of us grinning like lovesick fools when we broke apart. "Because you're officially stuck with me."

ACKNOWLEDGMENTS

I always kick off my acknowledgments with a thank you to you, my reader, and this book is no exception.

You have all waited so patiently for this story and I'm so glad you're still here.

I never expected you all to love Monty, West, Van, Stella, Bant and Imogen the way you have and I'm forever grateful for every post, video, picture, comment, like, share, email and DM you send me telling me how much you love these books and this series.

Chatting with you all is the best part of being an author. My gratitude is deeper than I can ever express.

To my ARC team - you're the very best humans and I'm so thankful you're coming along on this ride with me!

I have to thank my favourite writing gals — Steph, Ali and Emma — for their constant encouragement (and entertainment) when I was heavily pregnant, vomiting daily, yet determined to get this book out. And an extra thank you to Steph and Ali for their critical wisdom in earlier drafts of this story.

A special shoutout to mum, who reads everything I write even when I wish she wouldn't!

And to my family — Michael, William and now Johnny, who is the reason this book took so much longer than the others! — I love you. Without your support and willingness to let mummy write when she needs to, I wouldn't get to do this thing that brings me so much joy.

ALSO BY ELOUISE TYNAN

PIERSON U - SPICY COLLEGE SPORTS ROMANCE

WAITING TO SCORE

(Available in e-book, paperback and audio)

SHOOTING TO WIN

(Available in e-book, paperback and audio)

SPICY BULLY/HATE TO LOVE YOU NOVELLAS

HATED YOU FIRST

LOVED YOU FIRST - COMING SOON

ABOUT THE AUTHOR

Elouise Tynan is a romance author obsessed with stories about strong heroines and swoony heroes mixed with laughter, love and a little bit of heat.

She lives in Melbourne, Australia, with her husband and sons.

Visit her at:
www.elouisetynan.com
Instagram: @elouisetynanwrites
TikTok: @elouisetynanwrites

Made in the USA
Middletown, DE
26 September 2024

61540022R00135